I0736120

The Orchard

A Charlotte Wilson Mystery

Steven W. Booth

Los Angeles, California

Copyright © 2010, 2020 Steven W. Booth

All rights reserved. No part of this novel may be reproduced by any means without the written permission of the publisher, except for short passages used in critical reviews.

This novel is a work of fiction. Any resemblance to actual places, events, or persons living or dead is entirely coincidental.

Genius Book Publishing
PO Box 17752
Encino, CA 91416
geniusbookpublishing.com

ISBN: 978-1-947521-29-2

200418

To Leya
for everything

Acknowledgments

I would like to thank Eric Miller for being awesome and supportive, just in general but also in regard to my writing efforts. Without Eric, I would have spent a lot of boring nights arguing with myself, rather than engaged in witty repartee over story ideas, the concept of ambition, and publishing technology.

The Scribe Tribe, consisting of Leslie Ann Moore, Aaron Mason, Scott Herod, and Mike Robinson, deserve special thanks for keeping me company on many a Sunday as I worked on this and other projects.

And, without question, Leya, my beautiful wife, for not only supporting my creative efforts, but also for encouraging me to follow my muse. That she is my muse never really comes up.

Only small secrets need protection. Big secrets are
protected by public incredulity.
—Marshall McLuhan

Chapter One

"Are you going to let me see, too?" My eleven-year-old daughter had her nose pressed against the small side portal of the aircraft. On previous flights, I had been able to switch seats if I wanted to see the Rocky Mountains slowly slipping below us, but today the tiny cabin was filled with about twenty passengers, the capacity of the plane, and there were no empty seats. We were headed to Bozeman. There were rumors that the disease hadn't taken hold there yet. I guessed these people had the same idea that we did.

Samarie squealed with delight at each new feature. The rest of the passengers and I were treated to a running commentary as each new peak, river, and road came into view. I could see snow dusting the mountains as I peered over her head. The scent of her hair was strong in my nose, even through the cloth face mask, and I put my hands on her shoulders. Even though I wasn't very happy about being in a confined space with these people, I knew that this would be the last time I would see Samarie for a while, so I wanted to enjoy being with her.

"Look, Mom," she said, "That's the Big Hole River. Isn't it beautiful?"

"That's funny, it looks just like the back of your head," I said, squeezing her sides.

Samarie squeaked obligingly. "Mom!"

"Ah, there it is," I said, leaning past her and squishing her into her seat as I looked out the window. "You're right, it's absolutely lovely." I wrapped my arms around her, holding her close to me. I tried not to think about the months ahead without her. I didn't succeed.

The turboprop engines droned, giving a counterpoint to the sneeze of a passenger at the back of the plane, only a few seats away. As one, the other passengers and I turned to glare at the culprit. I was relieved to see that she was also wearing a surgical mask, but then she lifted it to blow her nose. Who knew what she was breathing into the reprocessed air?

"What's the first thing you're going to do when you get to the Orchard?" I asked Samarie, more to distract her from the sneezing woman than to know the answer. Samarie's mask hung loose, so I hooked the loops over her ears. I wasn't taking any chances with her getting sick.

"I think I'm going to ride Sasquatch," she said. Sasquatch was a particularly hairy horse, eighteen hands high and gentle as a kitten. Sasquatch followed Samarie everywhere. Her theory for his loyalty is that Sasquatch loved her, but I suspect it is the carrots she keeps in plain sight in her back pocket. Now that Samarie was eleven, I hoped she would use a little more sense when interacting with the indigenous beasts of the Orchard.

"Good plan. Maybe your father will want to ride with you down to the lake."

"And you, right?" she asked, turning from the window.

"You know I don't like horses," I said, hoping it would end the conversation. It was true, of course, but it wasn't the horses I dreaded spending time with.

"Ladies and gentlemen," came the pilot's voice over the intercom. "We're about eighty miles from Bozeman, and we will begin our descent shortly. We expect to be on the ground in about twenty minutes. There's some turbulence reported on our approach, so please keep your seat belts fastened until we have all three wheels on the ground and have come to a complete stop at the terminal. Thank you for flying with us." The pilot turned to look at the passengers from the little cockpit one row ahead of where I sat. I was surprised to see he wore a surgical mask, too, though I shouldn't have been. I reached for my phone, hoping to snap a picture of the masked pilot with the Rocky Mountains beyond, but he turned away before I could fish it out.

I considered getting up and asking him to turn around again to get the picture. Even if the network didn't want to use it, at the very least I could post it on social media.

"Wait here," I told Samarie as I unhitched my seatbelt and stood. The cabin ceiling was low, so I crouched as I made my way up to the where the pilot and copilot sat.

"Excuse me," I said as I tapped the pilot on the shoulder. He turned to look at me. I could see his eyes go wide as he saw my hand close to his face.

The copilot looked at me as well. "Miss, you need to go back to your seat," she said.

"I'm sorry to bother you. I'm a reporter for Foster Media in Seattle. I'd really like to take your picture." I steadied myself with one hand, and showed them my phone with the other.

"Don't you see the 'Fasten Your Seat Belts' sign?" asked the pilot.

"I know," I said. "This will just take a second." I held up my phone, as if that made it all right for me to be out of my seat.

The plane dropped suddenly, and the ceiling hit my head sharply. I reached up with my other hand to protect my head when the plane rolled. I lost my balance and dropped into the lap of another passenger, a man in a business suit. I put my hand on his shoulder to steady myself, touching his face in the process.

"Get off me!" he shouted. "What's wrong with you?" He rubbed his face, and I could see a red welt where I had touched him.

"Oh, God! Oh, I am so sorry, sir." I scrambled to my feet, eager to get away from him.

"You touched me," he growled, cupping his hand over the welt.

"Get in your seat," yelled the pilot. I scrambled back to the relative safety of my seat but didn't drop into it just yet. The pilot unfastened his seatbelt and went to tend to the man in the suit. I stood there, watching the drama unfold objectively, even though I was the cause of it. Remembering my phone, I quickly snapped a picture of the pilot kneeling in front of the suited man. The composition was good, with the mountains out the front windows in the background, the copilot glancing back at her captain, and a good view of the instruments. I snapped another one, just in case.

The pilot was speaking soothingly to the man when he glanced up at me. "Hold on," he said to him. The pilot stood, gripping the overhead compartments for stability, and approached me.

"Miss," he said sternly, "you need to get back in your seat. Right now."

I thought about confronting him but I remembered that Samarie was sitting there, watching everything, and I decided to comply. I sat and fastened my belt without waiting to be told again.

"Good. Now, when we get to Bozeman, you need to wait on the plane."

I could feel my frustration building. "Or what?" I challenged.

"Or I'll have you arrested. I wouldn't be surprised if this nice gentleman pressed assault charges against you."

I flushed but didn't say anything. I'd be much better off trying to talk my way out of this on the ground than trying to fight my way out of it in the air.

"Fine."

"Until this plane is on the ground and the door is open, I don't want you to move. Do you understand me?"

"I understand you," I said. I was angry, embarrassed. I could feel Samarie's eyes boring holes in the back of my head as she watched this all unfold.

"Good," he said again. Without another word, he went back to the cockpit and resumed his seat.

I sat there and stared at the back of the seat ahead of me. A small hand rested lightly on my arm. I turned my head and saw Samarie looking at me.

"I'm sorry about that, sweetie," I said softly.

"It's okay, Mom. You just need to work on your people skills, that's all."

I smiled. "Yeah, I suppose you're right." I leaned down and kissed her lightly on the cheek. "How'd you get to be so smart?"

"From you, of course," she said, smiling back.

Chapter Two

They led me off the aircraft in handcuffs. The Transportation Safety Administration officers were rude, officious, and callous. Samarie tried to protect me from the TSA people, which ended in her being taken one way and me being dragged another.

"Where's my daughter?" They had put me in a claustrophobically small interrogation room.

"Right now, you should be worrying about you." The officer in charge was an unnaturally skinny, tall man who reminded me of Abraham Lincoln without the beard. His name tag said Griffith. The room smelled strongly of disinfectant. The seat was hard and uncomfortable. The lights were harsh and glaring. They weren't going out of their way to make me feel at ease. "What were you doing out of your seat?"

"I explained that to the pilot. I just wanted to get his picture. I'm a reporter. It's what I do."

He scanned his portable, flipping through something which I presumed were his notes. "I don't see a release from the airline's department of public relations."

"It was just a picture," I insisted.

"So you admit that you were out of your seat taking unauthorized photographs." He tapped the screen of his portable. "Do you also admit to assaulting one of the passengers?"

"I didn't 'assault' him. I stumbled."

Griffith consulted his notes some more. "The way Mr. Anders explains it, you assaulted him. He's ready to press charges."

"You're kidding, right? The man has Witko-Byrne Syndrome. He shouldn't have been on a public flight in the first place. He could have contaminated us all."

"That's not your concern, Ms. Wilson."

"Not my concern? Haven't you seen what WBS can do to a person? The skin rashes, the debilitating pain, the infertility. Not to mention it can kill you. It's even worse in children. My daughter was on that flight. What the hell was he doing on that airplane?"

"Mr. Anders was wearing a mask and gloves. That has been shown to sufficiently reduce the risk of contamination. At any rate, I am going to note that you admit to the assault."

"I'm not admitting to anything. Do I need a lawyer? I wasn't Mirandized."

"The TSA isn't the police. We aren't required to Mirandize you, and you aren't entitled to a lawyer until you are formally charged."

"It sounds like I'm being charged to me. I'm not saying another thing until I see a lawyer."

"Ms. Wilson, perhaps you don't understand. This is a very serious matter. I suggest you cooperate. It will make things much easier."

"Easier for who, you or me?"

Officer Griffith's eyes smiled. The rest of his face was covered by a mask.

"I want to see my daughter," I said.

"Perhaps later. Let's start over from the beginning," he said. "What were you doing out of your seat?"

⁓

I was finally released late in the day. I threatened to accuse Anders, the fellow I'd "assaulted," and the airline of reckless endangerment and do an exposé on them. They ultimately decided not to press charges in exchange for my cooperation. Instead, they simply banned me from flying on that airline ever again. I'm lucky they didn't blackball me from flying with any airline. It's a long drive from Bozeman to Seattle.

Samarie, on the other hand, was treated fairly well—considering she was forcibly removed from me—and was allowed to eat something and use the restroom while she was waiting for them to finish my interrogation, a courtesy which they did not provide me with.

"I'm sorry you won't be able to ride Sasquatch today," I said to Samarie as we pulled out of the rental car parking lot. It was mid-afternoon, the sun hovering heavily over the tops of the western peaks.

"It's okay, Mom," Samarie said, but I could tell by her tone that it wasn't. She was angry and I couldn't blame her; I would have been too.

"No, it's not," I said. "Tell you what. If you want, tomorrow after breakfast, you and I can go riding all around the Orchard. How does that sound?"

The anger disappeared quickly. "You mean it? You'll really go riding with me?"

"I'll really go riding with you," I said, laying my hand on her knee.

"And Daddy can come too?"

I hesitated. I had been dreading seeing Warren since I'd decided to take Samarie back to Bozeman. Warren and I fought over everything, beginning and ending with custody of Samarie. I had her during the school months, and Warren had custody during the summers. But with the schools closing like they were, I couldn't look after her all day and work. Finding a nanny was not an option—it was too risky bringing strangers into the house. I had no choice but to send her to the Orchard for the time being. Besides, it was safer for her to be away from populated areas, at least until they could figure out what to do about all the sick people.

"Of course your father can come with us," I said finally.

"Yay!" she shouted, much too loudly in the small car.

The mountain roads twisted back and forth, making the underpowered economy car feel a bit like a racer, but not enough to make it fun. The sun was now well behind the mountains, and the car's automatic lights flicked on, illuminating the road ahead. Trees rushed by the outside of the headlights' beams, making ghostly images in the semi-darkness.

"I can't wait to see Paige," Samarie said. "I miss her something awful."

"You just saw her a month ago, silly head," I said.

"I know, but they don't have computers, and no one has a mobile phone either, so I can't talk to her or anything."

"Have you ever heard of writing her a letter? The Post Office is still working, last time I checked."

"Not to the Orchard it's not. They stopped delivering in May. You have to send everything FedEx now, and even that takes forever."

"Well, you'll be seeing her in about half an hour, so I wouldn't worry about saving your pennies for courier service."

We drove a while in silence. After all, we had already said just about everything there was to say to each other on the plane.

The road undulated wildly, challenging the engine and suspension of the little rental car, and making me wonder if I would make it back to Bozeman. I wished I could see the mountains—it would have made the drive at least a little interesting—but instead there were only trees for miles upon miles.

A small road-side sign appeared around a curve, and I slowed the car. "No Trespassing," it read.

"There it is," Samarie called out.

I turned onto a small dirt road and stopped in front of a large steel gate topped with spikes and razor wire. They were serious about keeping people out.

"Go open the lock, please."

"Sure." She jumped out of the car. I could see her tap a certain sequence of numbers on the combination lock, and the chain came apart. I decided to let Samarie push the gate open by herself. She was pretty wound up at this point, and I was hoping she would wear herself down so that she could get some sleep later. Actually, I was hoping I could get some sleep soon. Let her father deal with her being up all night.

In a moment, she had the gate open, and I drove through. Without prompting, Samarie closed the gate and locked it behind me. She hopped back into the car and slammed the door.

I started up the steep dirt road, the car struggling under its own weight.

The entrance road to the Orchard always reminded me of Donner Pass. I often had nightmares about getting stuck between two peaks with no way up or down, and being eaten by Samarie and Warren. I tried not to think about what that meant about me or why Warren would be there with us, but I'm sure some shrink would have a field day with that.

The car moved at a crawl as I picked the path out in the near darkness. Potholes in the dirt road rocked the little car, jarring my teeth and challenging my bladder, and I found myself driving a slalom course to avoid knocking out the suspension. I've asked Warren to fix that road every time I've come up here, but he always insists that the big biodiesel trucks they use don't have a problem over the narrow road.

Light peeked through the trees, and I had to remind myself that if the land here were flat, it would still be daylight.

"We're getting close." Samarie was already leaning forward, waiting for the first glance of the Orchard. A moment later, sunlight filled the windshield, and I had to flip down the visor to keep from being blinded.

The low sun touched the peaks across the valley, showing us the Orchard in all its glory. This place always reminded me of a huge football stadium, at least in shape if not size. The dirt road emptied out at approximately the fifty-yard line on the east side of the valley, which was essentially a large bowl with a river running through the middle of it, about two miles long and a mile wide. At the center of the valley was a somewhat large lake filled with sparkling clear, unnaturally cold water, and stocked with enough fish to keep a dedicated fisherman busy for years. In the north, from about the thirty-yard-line to the end-zone, was the pastureland filled with fat, happy cattle that had nothing better to do than eat grass all day and wait for that special moment when they were led to the slaughterhouse. Apart from that and the occasional visit from the vet, the cattle had almost no contact with humans, regardless of the fact that a few hundred people lived a mile or so away in the village at the center of the "stadium." The village itself stood directly before us, a few dozen quaint whitewashed buildings, like something out of a Little House on the Prairie rerun. The buildings were organized in a grid pattern, like a small colonial city, perfectly north-south, east-west. The only thing lacking was a cross on the top of the large building that doubled as a schoolhouse, auditorium, and dining hall. I gathered that the denizens of the Orchard prayed privately or in small groups, but from what Samarie has told me, there are so many faiths here that the only time everyone prays together is at weddings and funerals. There seemed to be plenty of weddings, but I hadn't heard of a funeral here in a few years. People at the Orchard were a hearty bunch.

To the south and west, the actual orchard of fruit trees occupied from about the forty-yard line to the other end zone. They always seemed to have plenty of apples, plums, and figs here, so I supposed that's what they were, but I never bothered to find out for certain. All told, the Orchard was very orderly, very clean, and very peaceful. And, as far as I was concerned, if I had to live here for more than a couple of days, I'd probably kill myself out of boredom.

Some people standing close to the nearest building looked up as we approached. They seemed startled to see us. One of the men ran off somewhere, and appeared after a moment with two shotguns, one of which he handed to another one of the men. The guns were leveled at us.

I pulled the car to a stop. Before I could do anything, Samarie jumped out of the car and shouted, "Hi, Bobby. Hi, Frank. It's just me and my mom."

The men evidently recognized Samarie, because they lowered the guns and waved us forward. Dutifully, I drove toward them.

"Samarie," said one of the men. "What the dickens are you doing back already? I thought you went off to school."

"They closed the schools," she said triumphantly. "So my mom brought me home."

I ignored the "home" comment and smiled at the men with the shotguns.

"All right. Go ahead," said the man.

"Thanks, Bobby," Samarie said.

I went past the people and headed to Warren's cottage. He wasn't at home—probably out tilling the soil or mending broken feelings or something—but his door was unlocked, as usual, so we just let ourselves in. For people who are so paranoid about strangers, they sure are trusting when it comes to each other.

Samarie and I hauled her huge bag into her room and dropped it on the floor next to her bed. We stripped the dust cover off the bed, and she immediately flopped onto it. She turned over on her back and said in a contented voice, "I'm home."

"I beg your pardon?" I asked. "Should I be offended? What do you call that place you live with me nine months out of the year?"

"I didn't mean it like that," she said, backpedaling. She jumped off the bed and wrapped her arms around me. "I love living with you. It's just that Sasquatch is here, and all my friends, and Daddy, and I don't have to go to school."

"Ha!" I laughed. "That's what you think. Just because the schools are closed doesn't mean that you don't have to learn. I packed all your books in your bag. You'll learn with the other kids your age. This isn't a vacation. It's just a temporary change of venue."

She flopped back down onto the bed. "I don't care. I'm home."

"Yes, you are," a deep voice behind me said.

My heart sank and my mouth went dry. "Hello, Warren," I said without turning.

Chapter Three

"What brings you back to my neck of the woods so soon, Lotte?" asked Warren.

I turned to look at him. He was wearing a red flannel shirt, jeans, square-toed engineer's boots, and a white, broad brimmed hat, looking very much the cowboy. He also smelled like a horse, which completed the experience.

"Nice to see you too, Warren." I shook my head slightly. I hoped he would pick up on the idea that I didn't want to discuss our return in front of Samarie.

"Nice to be seen." He looked past my shoulder to where Samarie lay on her bed. "Hey, Pookie Bear, you got a hug for your smelly old dad?"

Samarie leapt from her bed and ran to her father, hugging him around the waist in exactly the way she had just hugged me a moment ago. Jealousy doesn't describe what I was feeling at that moment.

Warren squeezed her, and then glanced up at me below the brim of his hat. "I noticed you didn't answer my question. To what do I owe the honor of your presence?"

I sighed. "It's getting worse, Warren. They closed the schools. I wanted to get her out of the way, and if there is anywhere I could take her that's out of the way, it's here."

Warren nodded. "I told you that when you picked her up a month ago."

"What do you want me to say?" I asked through gritted teeth.

"Nothing. I'm just glad you finally came to your senses. Until that syndrome…. What do they call it?"

"WBS," I said. "Look, can we discuss this later? Samarie and I are hungry and tired."

"I'm not tired," Samarie chirped.

I ignored her. "Do you suppose you could offer me some hospitality?"

Warren grinned. "If there's one thing we have in abundance here, it's hospitality." He released Samarie and held her at arm's length. "Pookie Bear, do you reckon you could run over to Patricia's house and tell her she and I won't be having dinner tonight."

Samarie was halfway out the door when she stopped. "What do I tell her if she asks why?" she called.

"She won't," Warren said simply.

I waited until Samarie was out of sight. "What's the matter with you, anyway? I've been going out of my way to not scare her for the last few weeks. On the plane ride up here, there was a guy who was really sick. When I touched him he swelled up like a beet in a microwave. I had a hell of a time hiding that from her."

"Why were you touching a stranger on a plane?"

"That's not the point!" I shouted. I took a deep breath and began again. "I need you to take her. At least a year."

"It's really that bad?" he asked.

"Believe me, I wouldn't be here if it wasn't." I started pacing. "I promised her I'd stay the night and go riding with her down to the lake in the morning. But then I really have to get back."

"All right. We've got a cottage you can use. It's out of the way, just in case you… you know," he hesitated.

"What? In case I'm carrying a deadly disease? Fine. I accept your quarantine. Do you want me to wear a mask and gloves, while we're at it?"

"No," Warren said thoughtfully. "It would just upset the others."

"Well, we can't have that, can we?" I said sarcastically.

Warren pointed his finger at me and said, "Lotte, if you're going to be my guest, you'll follow my rules. Got it?"

"Yes, sir!" I said, snapping to attention. "Now, I could use some food and some sleep. I've had a crappy day." Under my breath, I continued, "And it's not getting any better."

He scowled. "I'll have Samarie show you where it is when she gets back. Until then… I suppose you should make yourself comfortable. I'll get our dinner started."

I chose not to say anything else. Instead, I went into the front room and sat on the sofa. I must have been more tired than I thought, because I dozed off almost immediately. My last thoughts were of being devoured by Warren somewhere deep in the mountains.

Chapter Four

Samarie galloped Sasquatch ahead, turning so sharply at the lakeshore that I thought she and the big hairy beast would slip and go down. Instead, they raced north along the water's edge, seemingly for the sheer joy of it.

My horse, prosaically named Bingo—the name was only slightly better than Trigger in my book—had twitched like it wanted to join Sasquatch in the chase, but I wasn't going to let it. I kept its reigns pulled back, firmly informing my animal that a walking pace was a perfectly good speed.

Warren rode by my side. He held the reigns loosely in one hand, controlling the horse by telepathy, as far as I could discern. For a big, muscular man, it was surprising how well he managed that horse. He had kept up a steady stream of innocuous chatter ever since we left the stables.

When I could get a word in edgewise, I said, "Samarie thinks she won't have to go to school while she's here. I'm counting on you to make sure she doesn't fall behind in her studies."

"Okay, I'll talk to Patricia when we get back to the village."

I darkened. "What's she got to do with this?"

Warren lowered his shoulders and huffed. "It's up to each family to look after the education of their own children."

"What are you saying?" I didn't like where this was going.

"Patricia and I are engaged. We were getting married next June, right after Samarie was supposed to be back. It'll be up to her as much as me to make sure Samarie does her studies."

"Back up. You said you 'were getting married'? Does that mean you're not anymore?"

"No, it means that we discussed it last night after you went to bed, and we're going to do it next week."

The pit of my stomach felt like there was a bag of uncooked potatoes in there, weighing me down, threatening to knock me off this stupid horse. I couldn't decide if I was angry, sad, or jealous. Probably a little of all three.

"That's great," I said. I smiled at him. If he bought that smile, then I'm a better actor than I'd given myself credit for. "Congratulations."

"Thank you," he said.

I filled my lungs with clean mountain air and exhaled slowly. It was supposed to make the tension go away, but it didn't.

Before I had a chance to say anything else, Warren said, "Patricia and I think Samarie should stay here permanently."

I was so taken aback I didn't say anything at all. I just gaped at him, my mouth opening and closing like a fish.

"I've already made inquiries to my lawyer. With all the shit going on out there," he said, waving his hand at the hills and mountains that separated the Orchard from the outside world, "we think the judge will agree that this is the best place for Samarie."

"You are not taking my daughter away from me!" I said. "The judge has sided with me every time. You don't have a chance at getting full custody."

"I think I will. You should be getting the letter from my lawyer any day now. And it's going to go through, now that you've brought her back here. Even you think this is the best place for her."

"You bastard," I said under my breath. "You would pull a stunt like this." If I had been close enough to him, I would have slapped him. "No. No way. It's never going to happen."

"It's already happening, Lotte. You might as well accept it."

"You know what?" I said. "Fuck you." It was juvenile and pointless, but it made me feel better for that moment. I spurred Bingo forward, releasing the reigns, and let him run. Maybe he would dump me in the lake. That would make the day complete.

I caught up to Samarie coming back down the lakeshore. "Hey, Pumpkin," I said. "Are you enjoying yourself?"

"Why didn't you keep up?" she demanded in what I guessed was mock anger. The grin on her face gave her away.

"Sorry. Daddy and I wanted to talk."

"About the wedding?" she asked.

I caught my breath. "You know about that?"

"Patricia told me," she said, pointing to a distant figure. In the bright morning light, I couldn't make out her features very well at that distance, but I could see that she was curvy, petite, pretty, young. Just like I was when Warren married me. At least he's sticking to type.

"Do you like her?" I asked.

Samarie cocked her head to one side, reminding me of a Cocker Spaniel. "Not as much as I like you," she said.

I smiled. Beamed, actually. "I love you," I said to her.

Before she could respond, my phone rang loudly. Ordinarily I wouldn't be able to get a signal in the Orchard, but with Samarie here for the duration, I had invested in a pair of satellite phones. I frowned and shifted in the saddle, almost falling off, and dug the phone out of my pocket. I activated it and brought it up to my ear.

"Charlotte Wilson," I said.

"Lotte? Oh, thank God I caught you. Are you still in Montana?" It was Nick, my cameraman and producer.

"Yeah. I'll be back in town tomorrow morning." I glanced at Samarie. From the look on her face she wasn't happy with the interruption.

"No! Don't go back to Seattle. I need you to meet me in Milwaukee."

"Milwaukee?" I was surprised. "Why the hell would I want to go there?"

"I can't tell you over the phone. All I can tell you is it's big. Pulitzer big."

"Okay. I'll catch the next flight. How soon do I need to be there?"

Nick was breathless. "Now. Or sooner. He's not going to wait forever."

"Who isn't?"

"I'll tell you when you get here." He paused. "Lotte, you're going to love this." And then he was gone.

I put the phone back in my pocket and looked up at my daughter. Her father was next to her. They were waiting for me to finish.

"It's work, isn't it," Samarie said. It was not a question.

"I'm sorry, Pumpkin. I have to cut my visit short." I turned my horse—not an easy feat, despite the fact that Bingo was supposed to be a kiddie horse—and started walking him back to the stables.

Warren came up on my left, and Samarie walked Sasquatch beyond him.

"You can't stay?" he asked.

I couldn't tell if he was being serious, or just torturing me again. "No, I have to go chase down a story. You know how I get."

"Yeah, I remember. I still think of you as that little girl with the big camera who was embedded in my unit in Shiraz. Your helmet was bigger than you. Remember when that Iranian sniper popped it off your head?"

Of course I remembered it. It was the only story about my time in Iran that I would let Warren talk about in front of Samarie. I'm sure he was trying to be nice, but reminding me of the good times we had together was an odd counterpoint to learning that he was getting married in a few days, and that he planned to take my daughter away from me. I said nothing.

"Tell it again," Samarie said.

I ignored her.

Warren said, "I'll tell you tonight at dinner, okay Pookie Bear?" Mercifully, he stopped talking then.

Part of me wanted to wallow in my misery. After all this time, I still couldn't comprehend his decision to resign his commission as a major in the Army to become a farmer, or social worker, or whatever the hell he was now. He had had the gall to demand I give up my career as a reporter to follow him to this God-damned petting zoo he created. Now he had the balls to marry someone who for all intents and purposes was me ten years ago. And he thought he could just waltz all over my parental rights. After all that, he could ask me to stay? What a jerk!

On the other hand, this story had me thinking. Nick had a nose for great stories. If he said this was a Pulitzer waiting to happen, I believed him. But Milwaukee? Foster Media had an outlet in Milwaukee, and they weren't exactly the kind of reporters who liked to share a story. What made Nick think this was our story, and not Anne King's or some other local's?

Before I knew it, we were back at the stables. I dismounted Bingo, who looked relieved to have me off his back. I'm not a heavy woman, but compared to the little kids he's used to, I'm probably not that comfortable.

"Hi, Paige," I heard Samarie call from just outside the corral. Another dark-haired girl, about Samarie's age, came trotting up on a black and white horse that stood at least twice as tall as she was. "Daddy, can I go riding with Paige?" asked Samarie.

"Sure," he said. "Come back when the bell rings for lunch, okay?"

"Okay." She turned Sasquatch and started to head back down to the lake with Paige.

I turned and shouted, "Hey, Samarie! Aren't you going to say goodbye?"

Samarie maneuvered Sasquatch back into the corral and stopped next to me.

"Bye, Mom," she said, leaning down for me to kiss her.

"I love you," I said quietly, privately, in her ear.

"I love you too," she said. And having done her duty, she spun Sasquatch around and galloped off.

I watched as she rode off in a cloud of dust and wondered when I would see her again. All I knew was it wouldn't be soon enough.

Chapter Five

I sat down in the booth in the small café. I wondered how Nick had found this place. It was a fifties-style setup, with pictures of Elvis, Marilyn, and Ike everywhere. There were jukeboxes at the tables, and the booths looked like they were stripped directly from the interior of an old Corvette or Bel Air. I signaled the waitress, who wore a silly pink gingham outfit, a little pink hat, and an intense air of boredom. She also had the requisite facemask and gloves on, to try to stave off WBS. That this restaurant was even open was a bit of a miracle.

After slopping coffee into our cups, the waitress wandered off to chat with a coworker, without even stopping to wipe up the splatter.

"What's so damned important that I had to fly thirteen hundred miles to Wisconsin to meet you in this dump? You said it was juicy. Come on, spill it."

He smiled, the big silly grin brightening his stubbly face.

"Well?" I prompted.

"It's Verigro," he said, as if that explained everything.

I waited. He continued to smile. I opened a creamer and poured it slowly.

"Aren't you going to ask me about it?" he asked, the smile falling ever so slightly.

"You're getting to it, I'm sure." I sipped my coffee. It tasted liked it had been burning for hours.

Nick huffed. "You take all the fun out of things, you know that, Lotte?"

I decided to take pity on him. "Okay, fine. Gee, Nick," I said with mock enthusiasm, "what about Verigro?"

The smile returned. "There's something going on. Something big. Peter Youngs wants to talk to you."

"Who's that?" I had never heard of him.

"Oh, just the Chief Operating Officer."

"Hold on!" I said. Nick shushed me and looked around as if CNN was sitting on his shoulder. "Hold on," I repeated, more softly this time. "The COO? Why the hell would he want to talk to us?"

"No, not us. He wants to talk to you. Asked for you specifically. Wouldn't say what it was. I doubt he wants to show you pictures from his last vacation."

I sat back in my seat, which made flatulent noises as I shifted. Verigro was the largest biotech firm in the country, maybe the world. It made Monsanto look like a high school chemistry class, and Du Pont look like a baking-soda volcano. If I remembered correctly, Peter Youngs was Verigro's rising star. He was billed as young, brilliant, and powerful. If he had something to say, and he had to tell it to an investigative reporter from Seattle, it must be one hell of a scandal.

"Do we have a meeting?" I asked, keeping my voice almost to a whisper.

"About two hours from now. Some restaurant on Third Street. He originally suggested he meet you at Lake Park, but I told him it was too cloak and dagger."

"Did you do a background?"

"Right here," he said, handing over his portable. I paged through some basic stuff: Verigro's history, its current stock price, its board of directors—and I stopped. Errol Foster—the owner of Foster Media Network, in other words, our boss—held a position on their board.

"Did you see this?" I said, turning the portable so that he could look.

"Yeah," he said, nodding. The smile was plastered to his face again.

"You know he's going to go apeshit if he gets a hold of the fact that we are following this story."

"If it pans out, it'll be the biggest scoop in years. He's got to see that the story is better for the network than whatever he's got invested in Verigro shares. He's always been a health food kinda guy. Not exactly a biotech fanatic." He took a sip of his coffee and lowered his eyes. "Besides," he said into the cup, "you can always sweet-talk him into running it."

"Nick," I said, raising my voice again, "I've told you before to drop it. Foster and I haven't had anything to do with each other in years. I doubt I could sweet-talk him into checking his watch."

"All right," he said. "I'm sorry."

I glowered at him, then went back to paging through Nick's research. Verigro began as a participant in the Human Genome Project back in the 1990s. Fifteen years ago, they pioneered the technology for selective codon sequencing of DNA, which allowed them to write codons to order. They could now insert foreign genes precisely into the DNA sequence of nearly any organism and do it cheaply. If it came down to it, they could rewrite the entire genome of an organism from the files they had in their database. I kept waiting for them to start programming Tyrannosaurs, but that wasn't the business they were in. They made transgenic foods—mostly crops, but some transgenic animals as well—economical and safe, with little chance of replicative fading. Verigro's flagship product was BioStar, a gene from some unpronounceable thermophilic deep-sea bacteria which programs crops to stay fresh without refrigeration and maintain the nutritional value of foods after cooking. BioStar was hailed as a miracle, especially in third world counties. No more famine. Verigro was the hero of the biotech world.

"You think it's about BioStar?" I asked. The waitress approached to refill our coffee cups, and Nick leaned back in the booth as nonchalantly as he could muster.

Once the waitress had retreated behind the counter, Nick moved forward again, conspiratorially. "Yeah, I do," he said simply.

I looked at him for a moment, trying to remember. "Isn't their CEO running for Senate?"

"Yeah, Jackie Hughes is the front-runner, and is supposed to win in a landslide."

"If we run this story, it will destroy Hughes's political career."

"Yep," Nick said.

"Fuck," I said quietly. If there was something wrong with BioStar, then this really was a Pulitzer waiting to happen.

"I know the feeling," Nick said.

"The meeting's in two hours you said?"

"Yeah. Macchione's Italian Garden. Just you two."

"But you got us a truck, right? In case he wants to talk on the record?"

"No. No truck. We're flying under the radar on this one."

"What do you mean, no truck? Didn't you get this cleared with Jared?" Jared was our news director in Seattle.

"Nope. I wanted to see what we had before I stuck our necks out. There is a small but real chance that Youngs just wants to air some corporate dirty laundry."

"You unmitigated ass," I said, and I meant it. "Your plan was to get the story, then have me use my feminine wiles to persuade Foster to run a piece that could possibly cost him several million dollars in stock? Is that about right?"

"Well, when you put it that way…" he trailed off.

"You have to tell Jared. Call him right now!" I commanded.

"Look, Lotte. I'm the producer. This is my call. If we screw up, it will be my ass, not yours. You have to trust me, okay?"

I sighed. I seemed to be doing that a lot lately. "I do trust you, Nick. But this is crazy, even for you."

"I'll take that as a compliment," he said, the smile returning.

"Did you at least get me a hotel room? I'll need to freshen up before I meet with Youngs."

"Next door." I looked out the window to see a large, modern-looking hotel. "Parking's underground. The key is waiting at the front desk. I brought you a suit. It's in your room."

"At least you did something right," I grumbled.

"I heard that," Nick said sweetly.

I headed for my car with visions of a shower and a quick nap in my future.

Chapter Six

The suit Nick brought me was actually more of a cocktail dress, deep red with sequins here and there. It was flattering, sure—I've managed to keep in shape, despite being thirty-eight years old and a mother—but this wasn't a party or a fundraiser. Nick explained that he wanted it to look like a date, not an exclusive, and I could see his point. The shoes he brought weren't exactly stilettos, but the heels were fairly tall, not quite uncomfortably so. Diamond earrings finished the ensemble. The small wireless camera I wore over my ear was a little incongruous, but it looked enough like a wireless phone headset that at worst it would come across as pretentious and not silly. The receiver for the camera was in fact my phone—it's amazing how much they can cram into those little things nowadays—so no one would be the wiser if I got a call for some reason. I checked the reception and the view from my right ear, and declared myself ready to meet Peter Youngs.

Macchione's Italian Garden was set in the side of a mall, flanked by a frozen yogurt store and a bookshop. I felt slightly overdressed walking across the parking lot, but I wasn't really worried about anyone's opinion of me, except Peter's.

I looked at the picture of Youngs that Nick had supplied me with. A quick scan of the restaurant revealed one likely candidate. He sat in a booth in the middle of the room—not stuck in the corner with his back to the wall, as I've seen too many times—and I approached him. The picture showed Youngs in a beard, but this fellow had shaved recently. Oh, well. The worst that would happen if I was wrong is that I would have to keep looking. I noted that he wasn't wearing a mask or gloves, but neither were many of the other patrons. Apart from making it harder to eat, people who visited restaurants were the brave ones of the world. Those who really feared WBS stayed at home.

"Peter?" I said, smiling. If we were playing the first date, I might as well keep up the pretense. A few of the patrons looked at me, but I doubted they were doing anything but checking out my ass.

He stood and hugged me briefly. Apparently, he was on the same page for the "first date" angle. Still, it surprised me. Social distancing was a permanent fixture in society nowadays. Online dating had grown into a real industry over the last few years.

"Charlotte? I'm glad you made it." He wore a charcoal gray suit with a tasteful tie, and his shoes shined like mirrors. Still, not a two-thousand-dollar suit as I expected. I filed that away for later.

Peter was handsome in a boyish sort of way, with a roundish face and short, neat hair. I was surprised by the three days' worth of stubble. I rarely saw it with the corporate types. He looked a bit haggard. Perhaps that explained it.

I noticed there was a pair of wine glasses on the table, filled with dark red wine. Hmm.

I kept my smile, showing a few more teeth. "Of course I made it. I wouldn't have stood you up for the world." We sat, and I immediately picked up a menu. "I don't know about you, but I'm starved," I said.

"The chicken parmigiana is excellent here," he replied.

I glanced around the room. No one was paying us any attention.

I lowered my voice and leaned forward. "Thank you for meeting me, Mr. Youngs."

"Peter is fine," he replied, nonchalantly scanning the menu.

"Okay, Peter," I said. He seemed awfully calm, but I supposed that wasn't too surprising. Anyone who could rise to the position of Chief Operating Officer of a company like Verigro at thirty-seven years old must know how to compose himself.

The waiter approached, dressed all in black, carrying nothing but a smile. He took our order without writing it down. Pretty fancy for a hole-in-the-mall restaurant.

Peter sipped his wine casually. Placing the glass back on the table, he said, "I suppose you're wondering why I've asked you to meet me."

I smiled again, this time with genuine mirth. "I'm guessing you're a fan of Agatha Christie. I feel like I've walked onto the set of *And Then There Were None*."

"Actually," he replied, "I was never a big fan of hers. But if you are looking for a murder mystery, I think I can safely say you've found one."

Now he had my attention. I leaned forward again. "Are you saying someone was murdered?"

"In a manner of speaking, yes. But that's not what I am here to discuss. I want to know… no, I need to know, can you protect me?"

"Protect you? How?" I frowned, something I don't like to do, but at the moment it seemed appropriate.

"If I tell you what I know, there will be repercussions. Serious repercussions. This goes beyond keeping my name off the internet. Can you provide me with security? Protect my life?"

"Mr. Youngs…" I began.

"Peter."

"Peter, I don't know what you're mixed up in, but I'm not the FBI. I'm an investigative journalist. I don't do witness protection. I can offer you confidentiality, you can be sure of that, but if your life is in danger, you should go to the authorities."

"That's what I was afraid you were going to say. I can't go to the authorities. That would be like walking into the lion's den." He sipped his wine again. I noticed his hand was shaking slightly. "I understood that you helped protect that air traffic controller who blew the whistle on the FAA."

"Well, yeah. I did. But no one was coming after him with guns. All I had to do was put him up in a hotel room for a few weeks until I broke the story. After that, the damage was done, so there wasn't much for them to do to him but fire him, which would have been against the law. He kept his job and everything worked out. But that's not what we're talking about, is it?"

"Alas, no," he replied.

I blinked. Who says "alas" anymore? I studied his face. His eyes were sunken and dark. He looked like he hadn't seen enough sun—not terribly surprising in the northern latitudes, but this was bordering on computer-geek pale. His lips were pressed tightly together. He looked like he was depressed or in pain.

I looked at him harder. Did he have Witko-Byrne Syndrome? He didn't seem to have the symptoms. No visible rashes, no petechial hemorrhaging on his nose or cheeks. His gums had looked good when he smiled before. And when he embraced me, he touched my shoulders with his hands, and his cheek brushed up against mine. No, I was pretty certain that he wasn't sick. At least, not with WBS.

"What are you looking at?" he said after a long moment.

"I'm just trying to see if I can guess why the COO of the fourth largest corporation in America would be looking to me for protection. And why me? Why not someone from Chicago or L.A. or New York? Seattle is almost as out of the way as Milwaukee. Seems like an odd choice to me."

He cleared his throat. "Let's just say that I've always admired you from afar."

"Ah…" I said, relaxing. That explained the "dangerous liaisons" meeting, though not the crazy story about his life being in danger. "With all due respect, Peter, if all you wanted was to have dinner with me, you could have called my assistant. I'm sure we could have worked something out."

He smiled, but it was a sad smile. "While it would give me great pleasure to throw up my hands and say, 'Oh, you caught me,' that's not why I called you."

Right then, the waiter arrived with our food. He placed an antipasto salad in front of me, and penne pasta with meatballs before Peter. He offered to refill our wine glasses—I had not touched mine—but we dismissed him.

"So why did you call me?"

He hesitated, and looked at the small candle burning quietly on the table. "You are Warren Boyd's ex-wife, are you not?"

Chapter Seven

Who the fuck was this guy, anyway? I almost shouted, "What about it?" but I managed to keep my composure. So instead of grabbing him by the tie or splashing him with my wine, I said simply, calmly, "Why do you ask?"

Peter speared a penne with his fork and chewed thoughtfully. "Warren and I are… old acquaintances. I remembered you were an investigative reporter, so I looked you up. You have an excellent reputation as a journalist, by the way. I had to make a decision about who to trust. You seemed to be the ideal candidate."

"The ideal candidate for what?" I asked.

"To tell my story," he replied.

"And what's your story?" I tried.

"Ah, here we have come full circle. There is still one question that remains to be answered. Can you protect me?"

"From whom?" I tried again.

Peter hesitated again. "Suffice to say, people who would kill rather than be exposed to the world. People who have, in fact, killed many others without the slightest thought for their victims. I don't intend to be one of their victims. But they must be exposed, and I have chosen you to help me expose them. So I find myself in a quandary."

"Between the devil and the deep blue sea, I'd say. Tell you what. Let me make a phone call, maybe a couple, and see what I can come up with. It will just take a moment." I stood up. "I'll be right back," I said.

In response, he only smiled.

I followed the signs that said "restrooms" to the back—not very private, sure, but it was the best I could do. The double doors that led to the ladies' room actually took me into one of those industrial corridors that populate the interior of malls. Apparently, the Italian Garden shared restrooms with the frozen yogurt store and bookshop, and God knows how many other little stores.

I looked around for a quiet corner, and dug my phone out of my purse.

Nick picked up after two rings. "Did he show up?" he asked.

"Oh, yeah, he's here, all right," I said, leaning against the cold tile wall. "He's nothing like what I expected. Very precise, very formal. He actually used the words 'quandary' and 'alas' in a sentence. And the more I pressed him, the more formal he became. This guy is definitely hiding something. I just don't know what it is yet."

"Then what the hell are you doing talking to me? Go find out."

"Hold on. You're going to love this. First words out of his mouth were, 'Can you protect my life?' Like we can whisk him away to some secret journalist base with 24 hour security and machine guns."

"Hold on," Nick said. "Why does he need us to protect him?"

"He wouldn't say, damn it. Until I can guarantee his security, he won't talk. But I do know that someone was murdered, maybe more than one. Do me a favor. Find out everything you can about this guy, and do it fast. Start with a military record—his shoes were shinier than a new car."

"He never served. I'm sure of it."

"Double check anyway. And see if you can figure out how he might know Warren."

"Wait. Your Warren?"

A woman with a child covered in brown frozen yogurt walked down the corridor and headed to the ladies' room. As they approached, they squashed themselves against the far wall in an attempt to keep whatever contagion I might carry away from them. I waited until they were out of earshot.

"Yes, my Warren. He said he wanted me to help him because he's an old acquaintance of Warren's. That's how he knew he could trust me. Maybe they served together. I don't know."

"You must be joking. I don't know which network you think you're working for, but in my world I can't exactly access military service records. This isn't a cop show. There's only so much I can find out."

"Nick, this was your idea, remember. Figure it out." I looked around the corridor at the bright florescent lights. I prayed no one was listening, but I supposed it was too late by then. "This could be a great story, but it will only happen if we know what we are talking about."

"Okay, I'll see what I can do. What else?"

I tried to think if I was missing anything. "The other thing is, we have to find a way to put this guy's mind at ease. Maybe we can hire a private security firm for him. A bodyguard. That's your top priority."

"Wait a second. We have no budget for a bodyguard."

"Nick, if you had told Jared about what we were coming here for, we might have one. You're a producer. Produce something." Nick grumbled, but I could hear him tapping away at a keyboard in the background. "While you are at it, call George Martinez. Don't tell him anything. Just feel him out. After we break the story, we may need him."

"George Martinez," Nick said absently, as if he were writing it down. "Anything else?"

"No. I have to get back in there. Call me as soon as you have a lead on the bodyguard. Put it on my personal card if you have to. Just get me one."

"Got it. Don't let him get away, Lotte."

"I won't," I said, and disconnected. I went into the ladies' room to check my hair and my face. Finally, everything was in place. I headed back into the restaurant.

When I got back to the table, Peter was gone. My heart sank.

I flagged down the waiter. "Did you see where my date went?"

"Yeah," said the waiter. "He paid the bill and left."

"Shit. How long ago?"

"Maybe two minutes. You can probably catch him in the parking lot."

"Thanks," I said, and ran to the door.

I scanned the parking lot. Peter was nowhere to be seen. A few cars moved here and there, but in the darkness he could have been in any one of them. He was gone.

"Shit," I said again. So much for not letting him get away.

Chapter Eight

The next morning, Nick and I reviewed the recording of my conversation with Peter. Nick agreed, there was something wrong with that guy. But I still had no idea what it could be.

"Look at the way he sips his wine," Nick said. We sat in the small breakfast table of his hotel room, leaning forward in the uncomfortable chairs. He pointed to the screen of his portable, which was playing the recording back. "He's holding the stem in his fist. That's pretty odd for someone who is supposed to be sophisticated."

I frowned. "What exactly do we know about him, apart from what it says on the corporate website?"

"Not as much as I thought. He's supposed to have an Economics degree from Cornell. I phoned the registrar. When I asked for confirmation of his enrollment and degree, they gave me the run-around. When I pressed them, they hung up. And when I called back, the phone went straight to voicemail."

"That's pretty weird."

"Yeah, well, it gets weirder." Nick swiped his fingers across the screen of the portable. "His hometown is supposed to be Boston, right?"

"I didn't hear any Boston accent last night."

"That's probably because he's not really from Boston. At least, not as far as I can determine. I called Willie Bonilla—you remember him, the private detective in New York—and asked him to do some digging for us. He found all sorts of information on Youngs, but one thing stuck out. All trace of him disappears about fifteen years ago, and nothing reappears until six years ago, when he starts working for Jackie Hughes. Where was he for nine years?"

"Maybe he left the country?"

"Perhaps. Willie is still looking into his passport."

"How old did you say Youngs is, again?"

"His resume says he's thirty-seven. What are you thinking?"

"I'm still working the military angle. Fifteen years ago, he would have just finished college. That's a good time to recruit for Officer's Candidate School. Or the CIA, for that matter."

"That's not really helpful, Lotte. If he's CIA or something like that, there's no way we'll be able to track him down. It's an automatic dead end."

"Then that's an answer in and of itself, isn't it?" I stood and began to pace the room.

Nick shrugged. "Well, either he's a government agent, or Verigro is covering up something about him. Or he's here from outer space as a scout for our new alien overlords. Who knows? The only thing that I can confirm is that just over five years ago, he began his employment at Verigro, and less than two years later he was their Chief Operating Officer. Not bad for a couple of years' work, I'd say."

"So where the hell was he before five years ago?" I kept pacing. It helped me think. "What about George Martinez?" At this point I was fishing.

"Left a message. His office said he's out in the field and wouldn't tell me anything other than they would let him know I called." He turned in his chair and looked at me pointedly. "You know, you could save us both a lot of trouble if you just asked Warren."

"It's not like I can just pick up the phone and call him, you know. He doesn't believe in modern technology anymore. They make their own biodiesel out of God knows what for their tractors and trucks. There's a solar farm on the south end of the Orchard, just beyond the cows. They're off the grid entirely."

"I thought you said Samarie had a phone for emergencies."

"She does. But Warren makes her keep it off except for Friday nights when I call in to check on her." I sat down on the bed and spread my hands apart.

"It's Wednesday today. You'll call him in two days."

"Okay, fine. I'll call him. In the meantime, how are we going to track down our elusive Mr. Youngs?"

"You're an investigative reporter," Nick said, smiling. "Investigate something."

I chuckled. "All right. I deserved that." I thought for a moment. "I could call his office and see if they know where he is."

"Yes, you could." He took my phone from the table and handed it to me.

"In the meantime," I said, "find out where he lives. Maybe we can pay him a visit."

I put the phone on speaker so that Nick could hear and dialed the number that he showed me. The line was answered almost immediately.

"Verigro Corporate Offices," said a crisp, female voice. "How may I direct your call?"

"Peter Youngs, please."

"Just a moment, please."

The phone beeped and clicked. Instead of hold music, I was treated to short messages like "Verigro's BioStar technology helps make your food more nutritious and stay fresh longer" and "The World Health Organization reports that Verigro's BioStar technology has saved over one-hundred-million lives. With BioStar, famine is a thing of the past." Finally, someone picked up.

"Peter Youngs' office," another female voice said. It could have easily been the same woman as before.

"Peter Youngs, please," I said.

"I'm sorry, ma'am. Mr. Youngs is not in the office. May I take a message?"

"When will he return?" I asked.

"I really couldn't say, ma'am. May I take a message?" she repeated.

"Could I have his voicemail, then?" I asked. "It's personal."

"I'm sorry," she said again, "Mr. Youngs doesn't have voicemail. I'll be happy to take a message."

"Fine. Please tell Peter that Charlotte called. Tell him I had a nice time last night, and I'd like to see him again." I gave the secretary my mobile phone number and my personal email, just in case.

"Thank you, Charlotte," said the receptionist. "I'll make sure Mr. Youngs gets the message as soon as he returns to the office. Goodbye." The phone clicked, and I was disconnected.

"Well, that was rude," I said. "I guess we're going to have to find him on our own."

"That's what we do," Nick said.

"Yes, it is," I said. "But we're going to need a little help, I think." I began dialing the phone again.

"Who are you calling?"

"George Martinez."

Chapter Nine

"Charlie!" exclaimed George as soon as I had identified myself. "What's happenin', hot stuff?"

I winked at Nick. Here we go. "Thanks for taking our call, George."

"Our call? Who else you got with you?"

"I have you on speakerphone, and Nick is here with me."

"Hey, George," Nick said.

"How's it goin', Nick? Why wouldn't I take your call?" George asked suspiciously.

"Nick tried you earlier today, and they said you were out in the field," I replied.

"Oh, it's those fuckin' idiots at the front desk again. If you go to the head around here, they say you are out in the field." I chuckled at that. George cleared his throat. "So what can I do for you two on this fine October morning?"

"We were wondering if you could help me do a background check on someone."

George laughed. "Oh, come on, Charlie! I'm an FBI agent, not a private investigator."

"George, who caught that serial killer five years ago, you or me?" I asked.

"You identified him. I caught him," he grumbled.

"And who tracked down that terror cell last year?"

"Hey, that was a team effort, remember?" George hesitated, and I let him think. "All right. I'll see what I can do. Nothing deep, okay? Who is it you want information on?"

I smiled. "His name is Peter Youngs. He's COO of Verigro. He lives in Milwaukee. That's about all I can tell you for certain."

"COO of Verigro, eh? Why don't you just check the company website?"

"We did. We need something more than that."

"Has he done something that I should be aware of?" he asked. I could hear the wheels in his head turning.

"Not as far as I know."

"Then why come to me?" he asked. "Really, this sounds like the kind of work you'd throw a local skip tracer."

"We've already done that, and we came up with nothing. At least, nothing usable. Besides, we think he has a military background. You government types get kind of picky about who you let review that kind of information."

"Also," Nick said, "we think he may have changed his identity."

"What makes you think that?"

We told him about what we had discovered—or didn't discover—about Peter's timeline.

"I have to admit," George said, "that's pretty strange. Usually these corporate types are vetted pretty well. Okay, I'll look into it. Anything else I should know about?"

"Tell him about the other thing," Nick said.

"What other thing?" George asked.

"Hold on," I said quickly, and placed George on mute before Nick could say anything. "What's wrong with you?"

"He should know," Nick said flatly.

"If I tell him, he'll want to get involved. We might lose the story."

"Yeah, and if Youngs dies, we lose the story anyway. You told me to produce, so I'm producing. Tell him."

I thought about that for a moment. I had to admit Peter wasn't any good to me dead. "Fine," I said. I took George off mute.

"Youngs says his life is in danger," I admitted. "He said something about a murder, possibly several. He wanted to know if I could protect his life."

"Holy shit. Why didn't you come to me with this sooner?"

"I only found out last night. And he doesn't trust the government. Said they are part of the problem. I don't think he'd cooperate with you. He trusts me." At least I thought he did.

"Charlie, if you know where he is, you should bring him in. I can be at the Milwaukee office by tonight."

"That's the problem. I don't know where he is. I'm working on finding him. But I'd like to know who he is when I do find him. How soon do you think you can have that information to me?"

"I'll get to work on it right away. Do you have a picture of him?" George asked.

Nick jumped in. "We can do better than that, George, we can send you about twenty minutes of video."

I glared at Nick, but he just looked at me blankly. It was his call, and he'd made it.

"Okay, send that right away," George said. "Anything you have will help. I'll be in touch."

"Thanks, George," I said.

"No problem. Do me a favor, though, Charlie. Both of you."

"Yes?"

"Stay safe, all right. And let me know if you need anything else."

"You bet," I said. I disconnected the call and turned to Nick. "You better be right," I snarled.

"When was the last time I was wrong?" he smiled.

"I'm not worried about the last time," I replied. "I'm worried about the next time."

Chapter Ten

"You reckon he's home?" asked Nick as we pulled up to the curb.

"You never know. We may have gotten lucky." I stepped out of the passenger side of the car and looked up at the house.

Peter Youngs lived in a large house in Whitefish Bay, a few minutes' walk from Lake Michigan. There was no high wall or fence around it, much to my surprise. I'm used to corporate executives living in gated communities with armed guards at the entrance.

Nick came around the rented car and stood beside me. In the late morning sun, it was difficult to see if any of the lights were on inside Peter's house.

"Your camera ready?" I asked Nick.

"Right here," he said, patting a compact black object. I remember when cameras used to look like… well, cameras. The thing that Nick carried looked like a stick with a little black cylinder on one end and another stick coming out from that. The first stick was a shoulder stock, the cylinder was the camera with a fold-out screen, and the other stick was the microphone and light. The whole thing folded down into something that could fit in your pocket. If you didn't know what you were looking at, it would be hard to tell it was anything but, well, a stick, which often worked to our advantage when the recording started. "How about yours?"

I adjusted my headset, the same as I wore the night before. The recording quality wasn't nearly as good as Nick's, but as a "spy cam" it worked wonders.

"Already recording. Let's go."

Nick and I walked up to the front door. The door itself was high, at least ten feet, and rounded at the top. Heavy wood. Oak, maybe. Expensive.

"Try the doorbell," I suggested.

Nick pressed the center of what looked like a goblin's belly, but I'm sure it was supposed to be a cherub or something like it. The doorbell itself was loud, a gong that reminded me of the church around the corner from where Samarie and I live.

No other sound came from the house.

"Maybe he's not home," offered Nick.

I leaned over and rang the bell again.

Nothing.

"I guess we missed him." I reached into my pocket and pulled out my phone to end the recording.

The sound of a car approaching caught our attention, and we looked around the corner to see a black BMW, as shiny as Peter's shoes, turn into the driveway. Instead of continuing into the garage, he stopped the car and rolled down the window.

"What the hell are you doing here?"

"Hi, Peter," I said softly. "We never finished our conversation last night."

Peter looked around suspiciously. "All right," he said after a long pause. "Come inside before someone sees you."

He pulled into the garage, and we followed him. Peter led us into a large entry hall—I was sure he would refer to it as a foyer—with a high ceiling at least two stories up, and windows and skylights letting copious amounts of light inside. The floor was marble with granite accents, and the walls were clay brown. Tasteful—and I was sure expensive—paintings hung on the wall, and a large plant stood at the foot of the stairs.

He turned to face us. "How did you find me?" Peter asked.

"I'm an investigative reporter," I explained. "And I'm good at my job. Isn't that what you wanted?" I wandered around, poking my head into the rooms that led from the foyer—living room on the left, dining room on the right. "Nice place you've got here. Looks like Verigro has been good to you."

Peter ignored me. "You might as well make yourself comfortable. Can I offer you something to drink?" He led us into the living room and drew the shades.

"Water," I said, taking a seat on the leather sofa.

"I'm good," Nick said. He began to set up the tripod.

I took in the ambiance of the place—the art, the plants, the soft colors. The occasional nude gave it masculine impression. I made a mental note to track down his interior designer. They always know more about their clients than the clients themselves do.

Peter returned with a glass of what looked like Scotch and a bottle of water. He handed me the water, then took a seat. Nick pointed the camera at him. The light came on, and Peter lifted his hand to shade his eyes. "Hey, what are you doing?"

"Interviewing you. Surely you knew that we would want an interview when you contacted me."

Peter considered for a moment, then sat back in a plush leather chair. "Okay. But you don't broadcast a word without my say so. Agreed?"

I began to stand up. "Come on, Nick. Let's go."

"No!" Peter came to his feet and waved me back into my seat. "You can't just leave."

"Give me a reason to stay. So far all you've done is played games with me. Why not just tell me what is going on? You'll feel better once you get it off your chest."

"I don't know what you think this is about," he said, "but it isn't something that can be solved with a single interview. My life is in real danger here."

"I still don't understand what you expect me to do for you. I can tell your story, sure, but you seem to be able to afford your own protection. Why not just hire a bodyguard? It seems simpler than pinning your hopes on me."

"Are you telling me that you can't protect me?"

"I can protect your identity, Peter. I can protect your credibility. But I'm not armed and neither is Nick. I do have a friend at the FBI who would like to talk to you. Maybe he can give you the protection you need."

"You called the FBI on me?" He ran his fingers through his hair. "I can't believe this!"

"What's the matter with that?" I asked. "Have you done something wrong?"

"Don't you understand? The government is in on it."

"In on what?" I demanded.

Peter ignored me. He wandered around his living room, looking trapped. I could see that he was sweating. "Oh, God," he mumbled.

"Peter, just tell me what is going on. If you're blowing the whistle on Verigro, there are laws that protect you. And despite what you may be thinking, not everyone in government is corrupt. We'll find a way to keep you safe."

I glanced at Nick, and noticed he was recording the entire exchange. Good, I thought. At least we'd have something.

"You don't understand..." Peter began.

"Then explain it to me!"

Suddenly he stopped pacing. He took a swig of his Scotch.

"You really want to know what's going on?"

"That's why we're here," I said quietly.

He told us.

I stood there with my mouth open for a moment. "Now I know you're playing with us."

"I wish I were," he said solemnly.

"Would you care to elaborate on that?" I asked.

"It might take a while," he said apologetically.

"Believe me," I said, "I have nowhere better to be."

Chapter Eleven

"Mr. Foster's office. May I help you?"

"Oh, thank God, Marcy. I'm glad I caught you. This is Lotte Wilson. Is Errol available? It's kind of important." That was an understatement of the year.

"I'm sorry, Ms. Wilson. Mr. Foster is out of the office today. I can let him know you called, if you like."

I stopped pacing around Peter's foyer and looked over at Nick. I hissed, "He's not in." Nick's face fell. He spread his hands apart. I rolled my eyes in response. "Will he be in tomorrow?"

"He's not scheduled to be," said Marcy.

"All right, please tell him I need to speak to him urgently. I'm in the field, so he should call my mobile. I need to talk to him as soon as possible."

"I understand. May I tell him what it's regarding?" asked Marcy in a professional tone.

"You wouldn't believe me if I told you," I replied. "Don't forget to tell him, all right?"

"I promise he'll get the message as soon as I hear from him. Anything else I can do for you, Ms. Wilson?"

"No, that's it. Thanks, Marcy."

"Thank you. Goodbye."

I pulled the phone away from my ear and looked at it, as if it still held the answers I needed. "Shit," I said softly.

"So what do we do now?" asked Peter. He was on his third Scotch. He sat on the sofa, looking expectantly at me.

"I still think we should call my friend at the FBI," I suggested as I walked back into the living room.

"No! You can't call them. If you do, you might as well just send Jackie Hughes the tape."

"Okay. For the moment, we'll leave the FBI out of it." I turned to Nick. "How goes the editing?" I asked him.

"It goes," Nick replied. "I won't have anything useful for about an hour. You should probably make yourself comfortable."

Peter glared at me. "So that's it? We wait until he's done doing... whatever?"

"No," I said. "It's not that simple. If we're going to drop a bomb like this, we can't just do it between the weather and sports on the local evening news. We have to check sources, verify the allegations, back up your story as much as possible. That's going to take time. And it's going to need approval. Errol Foster is on Verigro's board, for goodness sake, and if we don't have his endorsement, he'll kill the story. If he does that, I won't even be able to write about it in my blog. Without Errol, we're done."

"And you're sure that you can convince him to run the story?" Peter asked.

Nick snorted. I glared at him. Neither of us said anything.

"What's that supposed to mean?" Peter demanded.

I glowered at Nick. "Nick thinks I have some special influence over Errol. Ordinarily I'd ignore him, but in this case, I hope he's right."

"What, are you sleeping with him or something?"

Nick stifled a laugh. "Not anymore," he said.

"Shut up, Nick," I snapped.

Peter leaned back on the sofa and smirked. "So you're boffing the boss, huh?"

"Look!" I shouted. I caught myself and took a deep breath. I could feel the frustration drop a bit as I said, "I don't need to explain myself to you, Peter. As far as you're concerned, Errol holds your fate in his hands, and so do I. I recommend that you keep giving me reasons for portraying you in a positive light. If we ran the tape as it is, you'd look guilty as hell, just like Jackie Hughes. So why don't you go take a nap? Sleep off all that booze you've been drinking. Nick and I will order Chinese or something. We'll wake you when the food gets here."

Peter opened his mouth to protest. Some unintoxicated part of his brain stopped him, and he seemed to think better of whatever he was about to say. "All right," he said. "I'll be upstairs." He stood up. "There are menus in that drawer," Peter said, gesturing vaguely to a small side table. He went back into the foyer, and I could hear him thudding up the stairs. A moment later, I heard a door close.

I sat heavily on the plush leather chair in which Peter had been interviewed. I sank into it and covered my eyes with my hand.

"Are you all right?" asked Nick.

"I'll be fine," I said. "No thanks to you. What the hell were you thinking telling him personal information about me like that? We have to look like professionals if we're going to keep his trust. Without him, we might as well be pissing in the wind."

"Sorry," Nick said. "I was out of line. It won't happen again."

"Nick," I said softly, "we've known each other, what? Thirteen or fourteen years. If you hadn't pulled me out of the line of fire in that rocket attack in Birjand, they would have been picking up pieces of me for a week. I know you."

"Okay," he said noncommittally.

"So why don't you tell me what the hell is bothering you? I've never seen you this jumpy. Come on, what's really going on?"

Nick sighed. I waited.

Finally, he said, "This is big, Lotte. I had no idea how big until Peter started talking. I thought this was a whistleblower over some corporate malfeasance. What Peter is talking about is murder, or at least depraved indifference. I can totally understand why he feels he needs protection. We might need it too."

I thought about that for a moment. Verigro had the reputation of being the good guys, the Boy Scouts of the biotech world. But if what Peter said was true, then it looked like they were as corrupt as any other big, politically-connected, multi-billion-dollar company. And I was just one phone call away from bringing them down. That would definitely not sit well with Verigro or its friends in high places.

"No, I suppose you don't. But that didn't stop Woodward and Bernstein."

"Woodward and Bernstein had Ben Bradlee backing them up. And they had Deep Throat feeding them information. What have we got?"

I smiled. "First of all, the reason Jared doesn't know about this story is because you didn't tell him."

"But now you understand why, right? He would have ordered us back to Seattle if we brought this to him. Jared wouldn't have the stomach for something like this."

I huffed. "Yeah, I suppose you're right." I reached forward and took Peter's nearly-empty glass of Scotch off the table and swigged down the last little bit. "As far as what we've got," I continued, "we have the second most powerful person at a multinational corporation basically telling us that his company has been engaged in the kind of corporate corruption that would have suited Caligula. If his story pans out...."

"If it pans out, then every politician who ever supported biotech since Ronald Reagan is going to look culpable. This story is going to make a lot of extraordinarily powerful people really unhappy." Nick paused, for effect I guessed. "People will kill over this," he said.

"Even if you're right," I said, "it won't be the first time people have tried to kill us. Back in Iran…"

Nick interrupted me. "In Iran, they were trying to kill everyone, including each other. And if you'll recall, we had a platoon of heavily armed, extremely well-trained soldiers with armored vehicles escorting us through the hot spots. If we play this wrong, anyone could come for us—a jogger, a grocery store clerk, the delivery guy bringing our dinner. We're exposed on this one, Lotte. And I don't like it."

"You're not going to start up about the black helicopters again, are you?" I asked, not very seriously.

"I am serious. And the black helicopters are real."

"Look," I said, smiling in a way that I hoped would calm him, "once we get Errol on board with this, we won't have anything to worry about except telling the best story we can. Errol's got more money than God, and he's just as well connected as Jackie Hughes and the other yahoos at Verigro. So there's nothing to worry about."

Nick said, "And if we don't get Errol on board? We can't sit on a story like this one. You know you can't."

I took a deep breath. "Let's deal with one thing at a time, okay?"

"Okay," he said.

I stood and walked over to the drawer with the menus. "What's it going to be?" I asked. "Pizza or Chinese?"

A loud ring came from my pocket. I fished out my phone and activated it.

"Charlotte Wilson," I said.

"What's so urgent, Lotte?" Errol asked.

"Errol?" I said. "Thanks for calling me back." I took a deep breath.

"What's the problem? Marcy said you sounded like you were in trouble."

"Not yet, but it could come to that. Are you in your office tomorrow?"

He paused. "For a little while. What's this all about?"

"Great. Can I come see you? I'm in Milwaukee. I can be in Chicago any time tomorrow. Or tonight. That would be better."

"Slow down. Tell me what's going on."

"I've got a story…" I began.

Errol's voice changed as he interrupted me. "Lotte, you've got a news director for that kind of thing. Go to Jerry, or whatever his name is."

"Jared would never give the go-ahead for this kind of story, Errol. It's got to come from you."

"Lotte, I'm getting impatient. Just tell me what's going on," Errol demanded.

I filled my lungs with air, and blurted out, "It's BioStar. It's toxic. And I can prove it."

"BioStar? That genetically modified stuff that Verigro sells? What, is it causing allergies or something?"

"Not allergies, Errol. Witko-Byrne Syndrome."

Errol was silent. I let him stew on that. I knew if I talked next, I'd lose him.

Finally, he said, "Be in my office in Chicago in three hours. And bring your source."

"Oh, he'll be there," I replied.

"He better be. You just bet your career on this story. You know that, right?" he snarled.

"I know."

Errol hung up. I took the phone away from my ear and looked at Nick.

"Well?" Nick demanded.

"He wants to see us in three hours in Chicago. If we leave right away, we should be able to make it easily. We're in business," I said.

"God, I hope so," replied Nick. He didn't look happy about it.

Chapter Twelve

I went upstairs to get Peter ready. There was an office and a guest bathroom on the right side of the hallway, and on the left was his bedroom. I tapped lightly on his door.

"Peter?" I called. "Time to wake up."

There was no response. I tapped again, and again there was nothing.

I opened the door and stepped inside. It was dark, but I could see Peter lying on the bed, still in his clothes. Good, I thought. At least that meant that it wouldn't take long for him to get ready.

I turned on the light. The bedroom was large, elegant, and well decorated. The colors were soft, a bit dark for my tastes, but it suited the room well.

I went over to Peter and shook him lightly. "Come on, Peter, we have to go."

In response to shaking him, he rolled over and curled up into a fetal position.

"Peter," I shouted. No response. "God damn it, Peter," I yelled. "It's time to leave."

Nothing.

I hadn't thought he had drunk that much, but he was dead asleep.

I went downstairs again. "Peter's not waking up," I said to Nick.

"Is he alive?" Nick asked. I couldn't tell if he was being serious or not.

"Yes," I said. "But if we miss this appointment, he may as well not be. Can you come upstairs and help me?"

"Let him sleep."

"We need to go, Nick. We need to get our stuff from the hotel and check out. Who knows if we're coming back to Milwaukee again."

"Errol said we have three hours. That's more than enough time to go to the hotel, get our things, come back here, and still make it to Chicago for our meeting. I'll go get our gear. That will give Peter some more time to sleep."

"And if we can't wake him up then?" I asked.

"Then we carry him out to the car." Nick began packing his equipment.

"All right. I guess we can spare forty-five minutes. Do you want me to come with you?"

"No, stay here and get some rest. I'll be back soon." Nick slung his bag over his shoulder and headed out to the car. The door clicked behind him.

I went back into the living room and sat down on the leather chair. I closed my eyes, not really expecting to fall asleep. I should have known myself better, because I was out within three minutes.

☙

A noise woke me up.

"Peter," I said, "is that you?" I stood up from the chair and walked into the dimly lit foyer. The blow came from behind, hitting me square in the back of the head, and I went down on the tile floor. I don't remember the second blow.

☙

Pain. Pain was everywhere. My head hurt, my mouth hurt, my wrists hurt, and my ankles hurt. My butt hurt from sitting on the floor. I was disoriented and dizzy, and it took me a while to realize that I was bound and gagged.

I guessed I was in the bedroom. Peter wasn't. I could hear some movement outside in the hallway. I hoped that whoever had tied me up had forgotten about me. It didn't feel like I had been violated, and I really hoped that I wouldn't be.

I heard some clattering and banging, which went on for a long time. I tried freeing my wrists and ankles, but they were held fast with plastic ties, and tied together so I couldn't stand or hop away. I was stuck. I sat there, wondering what would happen to me, what was happening to Peter, what would happen when Nick came back. I had no sense of time in that dark room—everything seemed to last eons.

Eventually a man came into the room. He was very tall. He left the lights off, and I could not see his face. The man peeled the tape off my mouth. "Maybe you'll be cooperative," he said. "Where's the key?"

"Please don't hurt me," I said.

"I hadn't really thought about that," he said, "but if pain is what motivates you, I'll consider it. Before we get there, why don't you just tell me where the key is?"

"I don't know what you mean," I said. "What key?"

"What's your name?" he asked.

"Charlotte," I said.

"Well, Charlotte, here's the way this is going to work. I ask questions, you give answers. Right now, the question is where is the key? Very soon, the question may be, are you willing to die to protect the key? If you answer the first question correctly, we won't have to consider the second question."

I didn't like the sound of that one bit. "I swear I don't know what you're talking about," I said. "I don't know what the key is, or where it might be. You have to believe me." I wasn't quite as scared as I made it out to be, but I was getting there. I figured honesty was the best choice.

"This is not a good start to our relationship, Charlotte. I'm going to give you one more chance. Where is the key?"

"I promise you, I don't know!"

The man shook his head. "You know what, Charlotte? I believe you. Which is unfortunate for you." He pulled something out of his pocket, and I could see that it was a folding knife, which he thumbed open. "Your role in this scenario has just changed." He walked toward me, brandishing the knife.

"No," I said, squirming. "Please, don't kill me."

"Shut up, Charlotte," he said simply. He moved toward me, kneeling, and cut the plastic tie that held my wrists and ankles together. "Stand up," he said, lifting me by an arm. I stood. "Come with me." He began pulling me forward.

I couldn't walk, so I had to hop to keep from falling over. The man led me into the office across the hall, where Peter was tied to a chair. He had been beaten and his face was a bloody mess. Someone had obviously been working on Peter for quite a while. He was also bleeding from the stomach. It looked bad.

"Charlotte," Peter said breathlessly. "Are you all right?"

"Shut up, Youngs," said the man. I had a good look at his face now—shaved head, straight nose, muscular build. This did not make me feel any better. If I could identify him, I was much more dangerous to him than when I was in the dark.

"Now," said the man, "you two have yourselves a problem. I want the key, and I'm going to get it. Therefore, this is what is going to happen. I'm going to ask you again," he said to Peter, "where the key is. If you don't tell me, or if you lie, I'm going to cut Charlotte here. Charlotte really doesn't want you to lie. So let's begin. Where is the key, Youngs?"

Peter stared at me wide-eyed. I didn't know what he would do, and I began shaking uncontrollably.

"Five more seconds, Youngs. Where do you think I should cut her first?" He held the knife up to my face.

"All right," Peter said. "I'll tell you. It's in the top drawer there." He nodded at the desk beside him. The man took the knife away from my face and stepped over to the desk. He rummaged through the desk drawer.

"Nice try," said the man. He took a step toward me with the knife.

At that moment, the doorbell rang. I could hear Nick's voice calling my name.

"What's that?" he asked me.

"My cameraman."

"Cameraman? What are you, a reporter?"

"Yes, and people will notice if I'm killed or disappear. Lots of people."

"Fuck," said the man. He hesitated a moment. Then he bent down.

"Oh, God!" I exclaimed.

"Shut up," said the man. He cut the plastic ties binding my ankles. Then he grabbed me by the elbow and marched me down the stairs. Before we got to the front door, he said, "Make him go away."

"How am I…?" I began, but he held the knife up to my throat. I had to think of something.

"Peter? Lotte?" called Nick again. He pounded on the door again.

"Nicholas?" I called.

"Lotte? What's going on? Open the door."

"Now's not a really good time for us, Nicholas. Maybe you can stop by tomorrow."

"Tomorrow? Lotte, is everything all right?"

"Everything's great," I said. "Peter and I just need a little alone time, that's all. You know." The man tightened his grip. I tried not to cry out.

"Okay," Nick said. "I guess I'll see you tomorrow." And then there was silence on the other side of the door.

The man dragged me upstairs and pushed me back into the office. "Now, where were we? Oh, yes. I was about to cut the lovely Charlotte."

"No!" cried Peter. "Don't. You just weren't looking hard enough. It's in the drawer, I swear!"

The man thought about it for a long moment. "You better be telling the truth," he said. He went back to the drawer and pulled it out of the desk. He dumped it on the desktop and began sifting through the contents. "I don't see it," he said.

Nick hit him hard and fast. They struggled and went down on the floor. They fought for the knife. The man punched Nick once, twice, and then got control of the knife again.

I stepped forward and kicked the man in the face as hard as I could. He didn't go unconscious like I thought he would. Instead, he stood and fled the room.

Nick followed him downstairs. A long time later, I heard the screech of tires. Nick's footsteps were loud on the stairs, and he burst back into the office out of breath.

"Oh, my God," he said. "What happened?"

"I don't know. Peter's hurt. Call 9-1-1."

"In a minute." He pulled out his pocketknife and cut my restraints. Then he went over to Peter to cut him free.

Nick was standing over Peter with a knife when the armed security officers came into the office, guns drawn.

"Down on the ground," ordered one of the rent-a-cops. "Do it!" He turned to me and said, "You, too."

"You don't understand," I said.

I was dragged from the room and led to the stairs.

Nick was already handcuffed, and he too was being forced down the stairs.

Security guards shouted and raced through the house. Radios blared incoherently. The security officer who led me outside twisted my arm painfully. Nick and I were forced into separate cars.

That was the last time anyone paid any attention to me for a long time.

Chapter Thirteen

They kept me in a small, windowless room. A single camera watched me with its cyclopean eye, quietly recording me rubbing my nose. I don't know how long I was there, because they confiscated my phone along with my purse and everything else I had with me. I sat there and wondered what had happened to Peter, and to Nick. I hadn't seen either of them since the ambulance had pulled away from Peter's house several hours before. I also wondered when someone would come fetch me.

After a while, I put my head down on the table where I sat and slept on my arms.

When I woke up again, my arms were numb and my bladder was full, so I presumed I had been out for a while.

"Hey," I said, rubbing my eyes, hoping they were recording audio as well as video, "I don't know what's going on, but I need to use the ladies' room ASAP." I stood and approached the camera mounted high up on the wall—too high for me to reach. "Please," I said. I went over and listened at the door, but there was only silence. "Better hurry. It's about to get messy in here."

A moment later, I could hear the deadbolt on the door being drawn back. I backed away from the door just as two plain-clothes police officers—detectives, I guessed—entered, their badges and handcuffs prominently displayed. I noted that neither of them had a pistol with them, and for that I breathed a sigh of relief.

"Have a seat," one said.

I pointed to the door. "I don't know if you heard me, but…."

"You can use the head in a minute," he said.

"Ms. Wilson, this is Detective Simpson," said the woman, indicating her partner. "And I am Detective Sergeant Lewis. We're sorry it took us so long to get back to you. We had a few other things that were a little more pressing." She spread some pictures out on the table. The pictures were of Peter in a hospital bed, wounded but presumably alive.

"So he's going to be okay?" I asked Detective Lewis.

"How do you know the victim?" asked Detective Simpson.

"I was interviewing him for a story. Listen, am I under arrest?"

"For the moment, you're in protective custody," said Lewis. "We're just trying to figure out what happened."

"What happened is that one or more armed intruders tied Peter and me up, tortured him, and threatened to kill me."

Simpson smirked. "We know two armed intruders were there, Ms. Wilson. We caught you."

"What?" I cried, standing. "You can't seriously think Nick and I were the ones who beat Peter up, can you?"

"Right now, that's what the evidence is telling us," said Lewis.

"Well, then your evidence has a fool for a client. How does your evidence explain the bruises on the back of my head, or the ligature marks on my wrists and ankles, or the Zip Ties I was wearing when the security thugs arrived? How does it explain no bruising on my hands or Nick's? How?"

"Why don't you tell us what you were doing there in the first place," said Simpson.

"I told you. I was doing an interview."

"An interview about what?" Simpson demanded.

"Peter is a prominent figure in Milwaukee, and his boss, Jackie Hughes, is running for U.S. Senate. Is that good enough?"

"That's a nice cover," Simpson said. "Why don't you tell us why you were really there?"

I couldn't believe my ears. "You've got to be kidding, right?" I said.

"Bill," said Lewis to Simpson, "why don't you take a walk, get us some coffee maybe. I think Ms. Wilson might be a little more cooperative if you weren't breathing down her neck."

He didn't argue. Instead, he turned from the table and opened the door. He stepped through and was about to close it when Lewis said, "No, leave it open."

That made me curious. I presumed that she wasn't going to beat me up on camera with the door open, but I couldn't figure out what she had in mind.

When Simpson was out of sight and, I guessed, out of earshot, Lewis said, "I'm sorry about my partner. He gets a bit enthusiastic about his job. Now, where were we?"

"I was explaining my presence in Peter's house, I believe, Detective."

"Donna," said the detective, extending her hand. I had already pegged her for the "good cop," but this was a bit excessive. Nevertheless, I shook her hand. "Charlotte," I introduced myself.

"Come on, Charlotte. I'll take you to the ladies' room."

I stood. Donna led me through a few corridors, keeping up a stream of light chatter. "I'm actually a big fan of yours, Charlotte. That piece you did on interstate drug traffickers was outstanding."

"Thanks," I said. "It's always nice to meet a fan."

After a moment, we arrived at the ladies' room. It was a small affair, with just one stall and a sink, but Donna came in with me anyway. I wondered if she would have come in if there had been no stall, just a toilet in the corner.

I closed the stall door behind me and sat down.

"You know, Charlotte," Donna said, "it would really help us if you would just tell us what you were interviewing the victim about. We know that he's an executive with

Verigro, so we've already guessed that you are doing a story about biotech. What we can't figure out is why someone would want to interview a relatively boring executive of an out of the way agricultural company two thousand miles away from their normal beat. What could he have to say that is that important?"

I finished my business and stood. "I thought I already explained that."

"And we made it clear that we didn't believe you." she said. Her friendly tone was gone.

I opened the stall door and moved to the sink. "Look at it from my perspective," I said as I washed my hands. "Either what happened to Peter Youngs has nothing to do with my story, in which case it doesn't matter what I was interviewing him about. Or someone attempted to murder my source for an important story, in which case the correct thing to do is not give in to that kind of intimidation and do everything I can to run the report."

"Why don't you look at it from our perspective, Charlotte," Donna said gruffly. "A man was tortured and nearly killed, and until we have someone else to focus on, you and your friend Nick are our prime suspects. We'd rather not waste our time with you, but right now, you're the key to this crime. Save us some trouble sifting through your personal life, and just tell us what was going on."

"If that's the way you feel about it, Detective," I said, using her title deliberately, "I'm done talking. And if I'm under arrest, I want to see a lawyer. End of conversation."

In retrospect, taking a hard line about cooperating was probably the wrong response.

Chapter Fourteen

I'd been in lock-up before—more times than I'd like to admit—but it had been a while, and I was out of the routine. For example, I don't remember being issued a surgical mask and vinyl gloves along with the prison scrubs the last time I was inside, but I was getting used to the idea.

I was brought, handcuffed, to the overnight holding cell, along with two other women. One was crying uncontrollably. The other was as stoic as a statue—I guessed it wasn't her first time either.

The guard who escorted us was reasonably polite—she actually handed the crying woman a handful of sani-wipes before locking us inside the communal cell. Once we were locked in, she removed our handcuffs through a slot in the door and set us loose with the rest of the denizens of the cell.

I looked around at the women, semi-faceless in their masks, and they eyed me in return. I counted twelve women all told, including the three of us who'd just entered. Some of them sat on the hard, plastic benches that lined the walls. Others milled about the middle of the room, arms folded defensively, keeping their distance from us newcomers.

I knew how to act in here—keep to yourself, find a place to sit, don't ruffle any feathers, don't reveal any personal details. And most importantly, don't discuss what you were accused of. The cameras and microphones, set high up on the wall, were watching us coldly, waiting for anything that might be used against us.

I sat down and studied each face in turn. Not so much to assess who was the biggest threat, although that was certainly a consideration, but to see if I could identify the tell-tale signs of Witko-Byrne Syndrome. After the interview with Peter, I was convinced that it wasn't contagious, but WBS could make people unpredictable, paranoid of any kind of physical contact, and they could be violent in protecting their personal space. Those who were not affected could be just as paranoid. Since there was no known cause of WBS—generally known, that is; I knew differently, of course—everyone, including most of the medical professionals, presumed it could be contagious, and public gatherings were almost a thing of the past.

Except in situations where it was impossible to avoid. Like air travel. Like prison.

My breath was hot in my mask, and my hands were sweating inside the vinyl gloves, but I chose to keep the protective gear on, mainly for show. Only one of the women took off her mask—the crying woman I was brought in with—and that was because she began vomiting violently into a conveniently provided bucket. I guessed she was drunk, or on some kind of drugs. Either way, she was very serious about being sick. I tried to ignore the heaves interspersed with sobs, but it was difficult at best.

"Oh, God," the vomiting woman said, and she heaved again.

"Oh, God, is right," a large woman standing nearby said. She had red eyes and dirty hair pulled back into a ponytail. She was taller than me, and she certainly looked stronger than me. She went to the door and called out, "Hey, guards! You gotta get rid of this one. She's going to contaminate everyone here!"

"Keep your mask on, Hodges. You'll be fine."

"If I get sick from that bitch, I'm going to kill her and sue your asses for everything you've got."

"Shut up and sit down," called the guard from her station in front of a monitor. "And relax. You two are going to be in there together until tomorrow morning at least."

"You can't do that," said Hodges, with real panic in her voice. "All I did was rob that liquor store. You're talking about a death sentence!"

"I said, shut up and sit down. Neither of you are going anywhere."

"Fuck!" cried Hodges, and she stomped away from the door. She began pacing on my side of the room—that is to say, as far away from the vomiting woman as possible. "She's going to give it to us all," Hodges rambled. "We're all going to fucking die." She began pacing faster, and I could see her hands shaking. After a while, her hands clenched into fists. Hodges began staring at the woman, who mercifully had stopped heaving, and was now lying on the ground, still sobbing. "Put your mask on, bitch," shouted Hodges. The vomiting woman just looked at her weakly and spit some greenish liquid into the bucket. "Put it on," Hodges said again, slowly, as if speaking to an idiot child. She took two steps toward the woman, her hands clenched. I didn't know what she was likely to do, and frankly I didn't want to find out.

Despite my better judgment, I stood and got in front of Hodges. "She's not a threat to you," I said. "Why don't you take a seat?"

"Why don't you shut up and mind your own business?"

"If you're planning on hurting her, it is my business," I replied.

"Maybe I plan on hurting you. Have you considered that, smartass?"

I sighed. "Look, Hodges," I said, "tonight I was hit over the head, tied up, threatened with a knife, arrested, and accused of attempted murder. The last thing I need right now is to fight with you. So why don't you just back down."

"Fuck you. If she won't put her mask on, I'll put it on her. And if I have to go through you to do it, that suits me just fine."

"We don't need to do this, Hodges. She's not a threat. Look at her."

"She looks like she's got it to me."

I knelt down on the floor. "I'll show you." I took off my gloves, then my mask. The smell of vomit was strong, making me want to gag. I turned my head to take a deep breath, and then I put my hands on the woman on the floor. "Come on, sweetie. Let's get you a drink."

The woman on the floor screamed, "Don't touch me! Don't touch me!" She scrambled away from me, knocking the almost full bucket over. Vomit spilled everywhere, making Hodges jump back.

"It's all right," I said soothingly. "I'm here to help you."

"Stay away from me," she shouted, scooting across the floor toward the wall near the toilet.

I took one more step toward her.

She screamed.

"What are you doing without your mask and gloves?" shouted someone from across the room. I looked up to see one of the guards coming toward me, a club in her hand.

I backed away with my hands up. I really didn't want to get hit again that night.

The guard grabbed me and turned me around. The guard twisted my arms behind me, cold handcuffs were snapped over my wrists, and I was dragged from the holding cell.

The next thing I knew, I was being shoved into a small, dark cell. The light blinked on as the door shut behind me. The guard removed my cuffs through a slot in the door.

If someone had asked me, I couldn't have said what the hell I was thinking in the holding cell. I almost got my ass kicked by Hodges, the woman on the floor, and the guard. I knew I had a tendency to jump in with both feet, but this was ridiculous.

On the other hand, I was sick of being pushed around. It felt good to kick that guy in the face after he threatened to cut me. And if I had had to, I would have gone one-on-one with Hodges. All things considered, I probably didn't do the crying woman any good. But I had to try.

I looked around at my surroundings. I hadn't expected to have a room to myself, but I decided to take advantage of the privacy. I laid down on the cot and went to sleep.

Chapter Fifteen

"Wilson!" called a harsh voice. "Wake up!"

I rolled over to see a guard standing at the door to my cell.

"What time is it?" I mumbled, stretching.

"You've got a visitor," said the guard, a short woman with graying hair.

I swung my feet off the cot and stood.

"Who is it?" I asked.

"How the hell should I know? Come over here and put your hands through the slot."

I approached the door and presented my hands in the reverse of the events of last night. The guard clicked the cold cuffs over my wrists and ordered me to step back. Once my hands were clear, she nodded to an unseen partner, and the door unlatched automatically and rolled loudly to the side. The small woman waved me forward and walked me down the hall to the tunnel, a long corridor that led from the jail back into the police station.

About ten minutes later, I found myself sitting alone in another interrogation room. The guard had been kind enough to remove my handcuffs. A large, one-way mirror dominated one of the walls. Another of the ubiquitous cameras watched quietly from a corner of the ceiling. Again, there was no clock.

A long time later, the door opened. Nick nearly tripped over himself as he was pushed inside. The door latched behind him.

I stood and we rushed together. I put my arms around him, and he held me tight.

"Are you all right?" he asked.

"I'm fine," I said, pulling away. I looked Nick up and down. He didn't seem any worse for wear.

"Thank God," Nick said.

"What about you?" I asked, sitting. Nick stayed standing.

Before he could answer, the door opened again. We both turned to look at who entered.

Errol stood in the doorway, flanked by two men in gray suits. He came inside and stood with his back to the mirror. Errol towered above Nick and me, wearing jeans and a red long-sleeved shirt. His dark blond hair was perfect, and he had obviously meticulously shaved his strong chin.

"Errol?" I cried. "What are you doing here?"

"I was just about to ask you the same question," he replied. "The police tell me that you tried to kill someone."

"Does that mean that Peter is still alive?" I demanded.

"For the moment," Errol said.

The tension rushed out of me. "That's great news, Errol. We've got no story without him."

"That's assuming there's going to be a story in the first place," said one of the gray suits, a man of medium height, medium brown hair, and medium build.

"Who are these guys?" asked Nick, indicating the two gray suits.

"Your lawyers. You're going to need them," replied Errol.

I stood and said, "Errol, we didn't do anything."

Errol huffed. "Why don't you tell me what the hell is going on?"

I glanced up at the camera and the mirror. "I don't think this is the right time to talk."

The other gray suit piped up. "This conversation is privileged. They can't use anything you say against you as long as I'm here."

"It's not the police I'm worried about," I replied. "I don't want to alert Jackie Hughes to what we've got," I whispered.

Errol laughed. "Whatever you think you've got, Jackie knows you're involved. So why don't you just tell me what the hell is going on."

"I'd rather you hear it from Peter. Are you sure he's all right?"

"I never said he's all right," Errol said enigmatically. "Whoever got to him did a real number on him. He's lucky to be alive. He lost a lot of blood. He's not going to be talking to anyone anytime soon."

"I'll make you a deal, Errol," I said. "Get us out of here, and we'll go somewhere private, and I'll tell you everything."

Gray suit number one leaned over and whispered into Errol's ear. Errol nodded a few times, then said, "Fine." He nodded to gray suit number two, who left the room. Errol turned to me. "I see you're just as stubborn as always, Lotte. All right. We'll get you out of here, and then you have a lot of talking to do." He went to the door and followed the lawyer out, leaving Nick and me in the interrogation room.

Nick looked at me as the door shut. "That went well."

Chapter Sixteen

After another hour of waiting in a cell upstairs, Errol and his two gray suits managed to get Nick and me released. I can't even begin to imagine what that cost him in money and favors, but I wasn't going to look a gift horse in the mouth.

Thinking of horses reminded me of Samarie. She would be expecting my call later today. And then I remembered: that would be my only chance to talk to Warren about how he might know Peter. In all the excitement over Peter's revelation about BioStar, I never learned how he knew Warren. And if Peter was as bad off as Errol indicated, he wouldn't be talking for a while.

Errol escorted Nick and me out of the police station and to his waiting limousine. I expected a stretch job, but this one was a rather sedate black SUV. Nick and the suits sat in the back row, leaving Errol and me in the middle.

"Go," Errol said to the driver.

"Where are we going?" I asked. I glanced back at Nick, but he was looking out the window.

"To the hospital. I want to see for myself who caused me so much trouble."

"I thought you said he wasn't talking yet."

"We'll see," Errol said enigmatically. "In the meantime, you're going to tell me exactly what the hell is going on. No one is listening this time. What is it that you think you know?"

"Well…" I hesitated.

"Lotte," Errol interrupted, "either you come clean, or I'm taking you off this story and giving it to Anne King. It should have been hers in the first place. Now's your chance. Talk."

I glanced back at Nick, who was looking at me this time. I held his eyes for a long moment. Finally he nodded.

"All right," I said, and shifted in my seat. I composed myself as if I were on camera, as if I were reporting. "Verigro is the largest biotech company in the country, and quite possibly the world. Verigro pioneered selective codon sequencing, or SCS, which uses a completely different process than the older CRISPR enzyme model. SCS allows Verigro to build genetic sequences to order, base by base, which in turn allows them to splice in any gene into any DNA chain. Before SCS, gene splicing relied on enzymes to insert foreign genes into host DNA, or on gene guns that shot DNA-covered gold beads into the nucleus of a cell, in the hopes that the cell's own machinery would include the foreign gene in its own DNA. For the most part that worked, but there was no way to predict where the foreign gene would end up in the DNA sequence. This led to problems like replicative fading and toxin production that could harm or kill either the host or the consumer. Most genetically modified organisms—or GMOs—created using the old technology had a marginal safety record, and the differences between natural exemplars and the GMOs could be detected by animals, who avoided the engineered foods, and by people, who experienced significant allergies to the GMOs.

"Verigro's SCS technology put an end to all of that. Instead of inserting a gene anywhere, possibly in the middle of another equally important gene, SCS allowed precise placement in a DNA sequence. This is important because the DNA of any two organisms in the same species is different in subtle ways. The differences are called alleles, and it's what makes you look different from your parents, or your siblings, or the person walking down the street. All organisms have these kinds of differences. And the combination of these different genotypes creates a hostile environment for mutations, especially mutations like the introduction of foreign genes. But with SCS, it is possible to add the same foreign gene to the same spot on many, many different versions of a species' DNA. When the foreign genes line up on the combined DNA—as in sexual reproduction—the mutation is integrated into the DNA sequence, and there is no selective pressure to get rid of it. That's why SCS has been such a success. Genetic sequences created with selective codon sequencing can survive for hundreds or thousands of generations, especially when combined with other SCS-created organisms.

"Enter BioStar. BioStar is a gene taken from bacteria that lives at the bottom of the sea around superhot thermal vents. The BioStar gene is actually a series of genes that allows the bacteria to survive the heat without being destroyed. When inserted into the genes of a crop, it gives that crop the ability to withstand cooking without losing its nutritional value. Perishable foods fortified with BioStar stay fresh up to one hundred times longer than natural foods when left at room temperature, and when refrigerated, they can stay fresh indefinitely. In that regard, BioStar is a miracle. It means that fresh food can be shipped to areas of food shortage or famine and stored indefinitely—or at least a really, really long time—and it will not only keep its freshness and nutritional value, but the food won't lose nutrients when cooked. BioStar has effectively ended world hunger.

"And the best part about BioStar is that it doesn't cause allergic reactions. Not in people, and not in animals. This is almost unheard of. BioStar is apparently completely safe for all uses. There hasn't been one reported case of a negative reaction to BioStar in the ten years or so it has been in use."

Errol leaned back in his seat. "All right," he said after a long breath, "if it's so damned safe, then why are we here?"

"Because it isn't safe. Not really. There hasn't been a reported case of a negative reaction because no one has reported it yet. According to our source, Verigro started noticing a connection between BioStar and Witko-Byrne Syndrome about four years ago, or two years after WBS came to the world's attention. Peter told me in his interview that BioStar requires almost five years to build up in the human body before any symptoms of WBS appear. Witko-Byrne Syndrome is an allergy to BioStar, but no one has made the connection because not everyone is affected, it takes years to begin to show symptoms and, quite frankly, BioStar is in almost every food product in the world. There isn't a direct connection that anyone can draw between BioStar and WBS. That is, unless you are specifically looking for it. Which Verigro did."

Errol shook his head. "Are you telling me that Verigro is covering this up?"

I gave a short laugh. "I would, if I were them. Witko-Byrne Syndrome is a horrible disease." I put my hand on Errol's. "You know that as well as anyone. After what happened with Ashton…."

"Don't," Errol said, sharply. "Just don't go there." He stared out the window for a long moment, and then turned abruptly back to me. "Do they know how to cure it?"

"Yes…" I began.

"How?" he demanded.

"Stop eating BioStar," I said simply.

It was Errol's turn to give a short, barking laugh. "How the hell are we supposed to do that? You said yourself that BioStar is in nearly every food product on the planet."

"I didn't say it was an easy cure," I replied quietly. "There are still organic foods—my daughter insists on eating them and nothing else—but the supply is miniscule, they're expensive, and they spoil much faster than BioStar."

"So that's it? We're stuck with WBS forever?"

"Well, not forever. Since WBS patients are almost universally infertile—plus with the skin conditions it's not like they are having sex anyway—eventually everyone who is allergic to WBS will die out. Natural selection."

Errol began laughing. "Natural selection? Ashton didn't die of natural selection. If what you are telling me is true, when Ashton died Verigro had already known about this for a couple of years. Ashton was poisoned." His laughter stopped as quickly as it started.

I sat quietly, waiting for him to continue, but he didn't.

Eventually, the driver said, "Sir, we're at the hospital."

Errol only nodded. Finally, he said, "All right, let's go meet this guy. When I get done with him, he's going to be the biggest hero since Superman."

Chapter Seventeen

Inside the hospital, Errol did all the talking. It took him only a moment to learn that Peter was resting comfortably in a private room upstairs somewhere. Learning the location of that room took a bit more time, but eventually we were led up to the fourth floor by the Chief of Surgery—a Dr. Soldato—who evidently had the impression that a sizable donation from Errol may be in the works.

"Here we are, folks," said Dr. Soldato, pointing to a door. He pulled a chart from the small pocket on the door and read to himself for a moment. "Mr. Youngs is doing remarkably well. He lost a lot of blood, but after the transfusion he woke up and was alert for almost an hour. Apart from a deep knife wound to his abdomen and some superficial lacerations to his face, he's in pretty good shape."

"Can we see him?" I asked.

Dr. Soldato hesitated. "Well, our policy…."

Errol reached into his coat pocket and produced a checkbook.

"Our policy," he said, eyeing the checkbook, "isn't exactly a hard and fast rule. I think we can arrange something. Wait here a moment." He signaled the desk nurse to come over, and he conferred with her for a short time. The nurse opened the door and went inside Peter's room. "We'll be able to go inside in just a moment. The nurse is just checking a few things."

"Thank you, Doctor," Errol said. He kept the checkbook in his hand but didn't open it or produce a pen. The doctor continued to eye it. I thought I could see him salivating, but I'm sure it was just my imagination.

The nurse emerged. "He's awake," she said. "You can come in." She handed out gloves and masks to each of us.

I went in first, quietly, almost timidly. "Peter?" I began. "It's Charlotte."

"Charlotte?" Peter said weakly. He smiled, which almost immediately turned into a frown. "Who are all these other people?"

I went up to the edge of the bed and pointed. "You know Nick," I said as we entered. "And this is my boss, Errol Foster."

"Hello, Errol," Peter said.

Errol gaped. "You've got to be kidding me. You're the source?"

"Sorry to disappoint you," Peter said.

"You two know each other?" I asked.

There was a long pause. Eventually, Errol simply said, "I thought I did."

Peter began coughing and clutching his stomach. The nurse went to him and checked a few of the tubes and instruments. She handed him a cup with a straw, and he had a few sips.

"Nurse," he said, "I'm tired. Can they come back another time?"

"Perhaps you're right," she said. She gave a significant look to Dr. Soldato. "Maybe now is not a good time."

Dr. Soldato hesitated. "We really should let him get his rest," he began. I noticed his eyes slipped down to Errol's hand, where he still held the checkbook.

"Peter," Errol said, "we need to talk."

In response, Peter coughed again.

"All right," said the nurse, "everyone out."

We all turned to head for the door. Abruptly, Peter grabbed my hand and held me back. As the others left the room, he pulled me down to him. I leaned in close.

"Listen," Peter whispered quickly. "Back at home. My office. Marvin the Martian. It's important. Go quickly." He let go of my hand. The nurse shuffled me out and closed the door behind me.

"That was a bust," Nick said.

"I'm sorry about that, Mr. Foster," said the Chief. "Perhaps you can come back to see him tomorrow." He was still salivating.

"I think I've seen enough," Errol said, and he pulled out a pen. He opened the checkbook and began writing.

I stepped over to Nick and whispered to him, "We've got to go."

"What's going on?" he asked.

"I'm not sure. Let's get away from Errol, and we'll find out."

"We can't exactly sneak away," he replied.

I smiled and winked at him. "Leave that to me."

I went back over to Errol and stood nearby. Errol finished writing and tore off one of the checks.

Dr. Soldato looked over the check. I couldn't tell from his expression if he was disappointed or just using a poker face, but he did not look like someone who had just hit the jackpot. "Thank you, Mr. Foster. I can't tell you how much I appreciate your generosity."

"Don't mention it," Errol said. "Now if you'll excuse us." Errol turned toward me.

I leaned in close to him. "I owe you, too, Errol."

"For what?" he asked, surprised.

"For getting us out of jail. For bringing us here. For everything. I really appreciate it. How can I repay you?" I smiled.

Errol looked at me a long time. Finally, he said, "What did he say to you?"

I pulled back, as if stung. "Who?"

"Peter. What did he say?"

"N… Nothing."

He leaned in close to me. "I don't believe you," he whispered.

"He said he was sorry for causing me so much trouble," I lied. I held my expression, very much like the Chief of Surgery did. I hoped Errol wouldn't catch me in this lie.

"Uh-huh. You really want to repay me?"

I nodded.

"Do your job. Get the story."

"I… intend to," I stammered.

"Good. Can I give you a ride somewhere?"

"No. Nick and I will figure it out."

"Come on, I'll buy you breakfast. There's something I want to discuss with you."

"I really think…" I began.

"Lotte, I'm buying you breakfast. Understand?"

I nodded that I did. "I'll go get Nick," I said and walked over to Nick.

"What's going on?" he asked.

"Errol is taking us out for breakfast," I said simply.

"That'll be fun," Nick said. "I thought we had to go."

I shook my head. "One thing at a time."

☙

Errol took us to a café not too far from the hospital. It served standard American food, but it was a far cry from that fifties disaster where Nick and I had breakfast in a few mornings ago.

It turned out that Errol had something to talk to me about, not Nick, so he and the two gray suits found other tables nearby, but not close enough to hear our conversation.

The server brought us coffee and cream and took our order. "So what did you want to talk to me about?" I asked once she had left.

Errol stared at his coffee cup. "You know that this story affects me directly, right?"

"I know. Ashton…."

"No, this isn't about Ashton. It's Alice. She lost another baby."

"Oh, my God," I exclaimed. "When did this happen?"

"Two months ago. She and I decided not to make it public."

"I'm so sorry," I said, more quietly this time. "I know how important it is for you to have children."

"Not just children, Lotte. An heir." He put his coffee cup down. "It gets worse," he said. "Alice has WBS. We found out when she lost the baby."

I reached over and took his hand. I really wanted to say something that would make him feel better, but there was nothing to say. I finally managed, "What are you going to do?"

"What am I supposed to do?" he asked, shaking his head. "I don't have any choice. I'm bringing in a surrogate."

For a moment, I actually didn't believe what I heard. "A… a surrogate?"

"Yes," he said. "Alice is my third wife, and none of them have been able to bear me a living heir. What am I supposed to do? Divorce Alice and marry someone else?"

I was so shocked I didn't say anything.

Errol put his hand on top of mine. "You know what I can't figure out?"

"What?" I asked.

"I can't figure out why you turned me down two years ago."

I pulled my hands back. "Errol, there are a lot of things that I aspire to. Being Mrs. Errol Foster isn't one of them."

"Why not? I'm a good provider. Besides, I can think of worse people you could marry. Warren Boyd, for instance."

"Errol," I growled, "I am the last person to defend Warren. But you have to understand, I'm no one's broodmare."

"Don't be like that, Lotte. I'm not asking you to be anything you're not. Am I such a bad guy that you wouldn't even consider an offer?"

"An offer?" I said incredulously. "Errol, this isn't a business transaction. You're married. You're obviously still mourning Ashton, and maybe you're even distraught over Alice and the baby. So let's just pretend you didn't just suggest that you dump your sick wife so that I can marry you and bear you your heir."

"Hear me out," he began.

"No," I said, "I don't want to hear you out. You want to know why I never seriously considered your offer? Because with you, everything is business. I know there's a good, caring person in there somewhere, but if you ever actually let it show, I think I might fall over and die of surprise. I don't want to be one of your business transactions, Errol."

"Lower your voice," he insisted.

I leaned in close, and whispered, "Fine. Here's what's going to happen. I'm going to bring in this story, and you're going to give me a raise and a bonus and offer me my own national show. And you're never going to bring up marriage or children or surrogates or any of this to me ever again. Now why don't you go home to your sick wife and leave me out of your twisted little world?"

I stood and left the table. If Errol said anything else, I didn't hear him.

"Come on, Nick," I said. "It's time to go." Nick and I headed toward the door.

"You want to tell me what the hell is going on?"

"No. Just get us a cab."

"Where are we going?" he asked.

"Peter's house."

Chapter Eighteen

When the cab dropped us off at Peter's house, there were no police to be seen, but crime scene tape was over the door.

"The back door was unlocked last night. Let's see what we can do." Nick and I headed around to the back.

The back door was still unlocked, although it was officially sealed with a sticker announcing that trespassing was punishable by arrest and prosecution. I took a small pen knife out of my purse and slit the seal at the edge of the door. The door opened easily, and we went inside.

Peter's house was a complete mess. That guy who attacked us had trashed every room. Drawers were dumped out in the kitchen, and the living room was an utter disaster. China dishes lay everywhere in the dining room, many of which were smashed. It looked like a tornado had come through the house.

We climbed the stairs two at a time. Peter's office door stood open, just as it was when I was here two days ago.

That guy had done an amazing job of destroying Peter's office. Papers and computer components lay everywhere. Smashed pictures lay face down on the floor, and glass covered the carpet.

I shook my head. "How the hell did he expect to find anything in this mess?"

"I could ask you the same thing about us," Nick said. "You really think we're going to find this whatever-it-is in here?"

"Marvin the Martian," I replied. "We'd better. I don't know why it's important, but I don't think Peter asked us to find it so that he would have something to cuddle up with in his hospital bed."

I began scanning the floor for anything that might look like the elusive cartoon character. I stepped over the blood stains on the carpet. They looked dry, but there was no sense tracking blood through the house if they weren't.

Nick took the desk, carefully sifting through the debris. I heard him mumbling comments to himself, probably regarding the impossibility of the task ahead of us. I ignored him.

If the contents of a person's house are an indicator of their personality, I would say that Peter Youngs was all work and no play. The papers all seemed to be Verigro documents, and the pictures on the walls all seemed to be company functions. No family pictures, no childhood snapshots. No university diplomas, I noted. Then it occurred to me, he never actually graduated from Cornell—at least, not as far as we knew—so why bother with a fake diploma.

"Any luck over there?" I asked.

"Nope," replied Nick. "What makes you think whoever did all this didn't find Marvin?"

"He was still torturing us when you came in and chased him out. I can't imagine he found it, but if he did, we're screwed. And if he didn't, all the more reason for us to track it down."

"Unless the thing that guy was looking for and Marvin are two different things."

I started getting impatient. I began shoving handfuls of paper to one side, hoping that I wouldn't cover up the very thing that I was looking for. I could feel frustration building up in me. I didn't know how long we had to look and I kept thinking that if I didn't find our Martian friend we'd be at another standstill.

"Hey!" Nick said. He smiled.

"Did you find it?" I asked eagerly.

Nick held up a small round object. "Marvin the Martian, as promised." He tossed it to me.

I looked at it. It was a plastic head, missing the body, of Marvin. "Where's the rest of it?"

Nick shrugged. "I have no idea. Isn't that what we're looking for?"

"Beats the hell out of me." I turned over the plastic head and looked into the neck to see if anything was stuck inside. Instead of finding what I was looking for, all

I found was a rectangular hole, about a centimeter wide and three or four millimeters thick. It reminded me of something. "What does that look like?" I asked, tossing the head back to Nick.

Nick caught it and looked into the neck. "A hole?" he asked.

"I know that, smartass. What kind of hole?"

"I don't know what you're asking. It's probably just where the head meets the body."

"All right," I said. "Keep looking." I moved around to the front of Peter's desk. There were some more papers there, along with some other debris. I started shuffling through it.

Peter's computer, which consisted of a monitor-motherboard combination, lay on the floor. Two wires ran from it—power and something plugged into the data port. The other end of the data cable ran under the papers on the floor. I tugged on it. Marvin's decapitated body slithered out from under the papers.

I stood up so fast that I banged my head on the underside of the desk. "Ow!" I laughed.

"You all right over there?"

"Oh, I'm better than all right. Lookie what I found." I held up the decapitated bottom half of Marvin.

"Yes!" cried Nick.

I disconnected him from the data cable. "See, that's what I'm talking about. This is a data connector. I'll bet you a dollar that this thing is a memory drive."

"I'll take that," said a voice from the door. I turned to see a large gun accompanied by a larger man. He pulled the hammer back on the pistol.

I knew it couldn't be that easy.

Chapter Nineteen

"Toss it here," said the man with the gun. It was the same man who had offered to carve me up if he couldn't find the "key." His face was bruised where I had kicked him, and he had a long gash on his head from when he and Nick had been fighting.

I glanced back at Nick. He shook his head almost imperceptibly.

"Hey, look at me. Remember me? The man with the big gun pointed at your head." He gestured with the pistol. "Toss it here." He held out his other hand.

I stood there, frozen. "If I do, you'll kill me," I said.

"If you don't, I'll kill you for sure. Now throw it. Easy now."

I didn't feel like being dead at just that moment, so I decided to comply. I lowered my arm and tossed Marvin's body to him. He caught it with ease.

"Very good," he said, smiling. He backed out of the door. "Now come on out," he said. "Slowly. I don't want to get nervous."

Nick and I came forward. I left my arms loose at my sides—he hadn't ordered us to put our hands up, and I didn't want to startle him—and weaved my way through the debris on the floor.

The man continued to back up into the hallway, on the end away from the stairs. I proceeded out into the hall, never taking my eyes off him. Nick was right beside me.

"Let's go talk in the living room, shall we?" he said. He gestured toward the stairs behind us. "Turn around. And don't forget I have this gun pointed right at your back."

We turned and walked slowly toward the stairs.

A loud trilling beep came from the man with the gun. I looked over my shoulder and saw him draw a phone from his pocket. He pushed a button on the side, and said, "Go ahead," loudly, as if he were speaking into a walkie-talkie. He gestured for us to continue walking.

"Have you got it?" asked a voice from the phone.

"Yes," he said, "and I've got some company. I was just about to contact you to find out what to do with them."

"Who are they?" said the disembodied voice.

"It's the reporter and her cameraman again," he said into the phone.

I stood at the top of the stairs. I took a step down. Nick was right behind me, and the gunman was behind Nick.

"Should I kill them?" asked the man.

That was enough for Nick. He swung around and grabbed the man's wrist and pulled him toward the stairs. I saw the man's foot go out from under him, and he tumbled down the stairs right past me, right on his head. The gun went clattering across the tile floor. Nick went bounding after him. He kicked the man in the face, and I could hear his nose and teeth collapse under the blow.

"Get the drive," insisted Nick. He went running after the gun.

I checked the man briefly. I couldn't tell if he was dead, but he certainly wasn't awake. I reached into his pocket and retrieved Marvin's body. I also found his car keys and his wallet, which I pocketed as well.

"Miller?" asked the voice from the phone, which lay on the floor next to the man's hand. "Miller, are you there?"

Nick took me by the wrist and pulled me to my feet. "We gotta go!"

We ran out the back, leaving the phone to talk to itself.

The man's car sat in the driveway next to Peter's black BMW. It was a late-model Mercedes sedan; silver, shiny. I pushed the remote, and the doors opened.

"Let's go," I said, jumping into the driver's seat.

Nick didn't argue. He opened the passenger door and got in.

I started it up and backed out of the driveway as calmly as I could. As soon as I was clear, I drove down the street as if I were a resident—no apparent hurry.

"What the fuck are we going to do now?" Nick asked.

"We're going to go get Peter out of that hospital and take him somewhere safe."

"Somewhere safe like where?"

"When I figure that out, I'll let you know. In the meantime, find out who this guy is." I dug the wallet out of my pocket and handed it to Nick.

"His ID says he's Jeff Miller. Lives in Milwaukee. Brown eyes, brown hair—when he has hair, I suppose— six foot four inches, two-hundred-forty pounds. Jesus, what the hell was I thinking taking that guy on?"

"You were thinking we were about to die," I said. "Thank you."

"Yeah, well, you owe me another one." He kept scanning through Miller's wallet. "Seven-hundred dollars in twenties and fifties. Assorted credit cards." Those he dumped into the glove box but hung onto the cash. "Hello! What's this?" He held up a card.

"What is it?" I asked, not taking my eyes off the road.

"Jackie Hughes's business card. I wonder what he was doing with that."

I wasn't expecting that. "Well, what do you know? That might explain a lot."

"You think Hughes is the one who wants Youngs killed?"

"That's exactly what I think. They probably needed him alive until they found Marvin," I gestured. "After that, he's more trouble than he's worth."

"Then we'd better go get him."

"Any idea how we're going to get him out?"

"Not a clue. But I'm not worried. You'll think of something."

"Thanks a lot," I said.

Chapter Twenty

Timing was everything.

Peter's room wasn't locked, but it was under constant supervision by the desk nurse. That meant a diversion. A long one. At least 5 minutes, maybe more. And that was presuming that we could convince Peter to come with us.

I had reason to believe he would.

The elevator door opened on the telemetry floor and Nick and I stepped off. I had the tote bag slung over my shoulder filled with clothes for Peter we had picked up at a local store. It was busier than when we had visited earlier. Hopefully we could use that to our advantage. We needed all the help we could get.

Nick walked ahead of me. We tried to make it seem as if we weren't together. No one paid us any attention.

Nick went toward the front desk. I headed toward Peter's door. He looked back at me, and I nodded. It was now or never.

I watched as Nick approached the desk nurse and said something to her. I couldn't hear what he was saying, but he moved to the far end of the counter, making sure the nurse looked away from Peter's door. I heard Nick raise his voice. He played the unhappy customer to the hilt. A man in a white coat walked up and joined in the conversation. Nick waved at me, low near his leg. That was the signal.

I cracked the door open, took one last look around, and went in.

"Peter, we have to get you out of here," I said as I entered. "Someone is going to…."

That was as far as I got before I noticed the woman sitting next to Peter.

The woman was older—I would guess she was in her sixties—and dressed very nicely in a dark, fashionable suit that probably cost a couple thousand dollars or more. Her hair was long, fair, curly, pulled back into a clip at her collar. She had small, slender, almost non-existent glasses hovering on her nose. Her hands were folded in her lap.

"Someone is going to what?" Jackie Hughes asked.

I hesitated. I couldn't think of a convenient lie, so I tried a partial truth. "Someone wants to hurt Peter. I'm concerned about his safety."

"That's very touching, but I assure you, nothing is going to happen to Peter if I have anything to say about it."

I almost laughed. Almost. "What exactly do you have to say about it, Jackie?"

She looked at me blankly. "I don't know what you mean."

"Well, Peter's here in the hospital," I said, ignoring the fact that Peter was in the room. "Someone attacked him viciously. They tore up his house looking for something. Why do you suppose they did that?"

"I know you," said Jackie, frowning. "You're that reporter they caught in Peter's house. Wilson. Charlotte Wilson. How did you get away from the police?" There was a glint in Jackie's eye which I didn't like.

"I didn't 'get away from them,'" I said. "I was released. I understand the police now have another suspect in mind. I wonder who that could be."

"I couldn't say," growled Jackie.

"Then perhaps you could answer my question. Why would someone be looking for something in Peter's house?"

"I assure you I have no idea. But whatever they were looking for, I hope for their sake they didn't find it."

"Really? That seems fairly specific."

Jackie glared at me. She opened her mouth to respond.

The door opened behind me. A nurse came in, a short man with thick black hair. He didn't look happy.

"Keep your voices down!" he insisted. "I told you: one visitor at a time. I'm afraid you're both going to have to leave." He held the door open. "Now," he said.

I went out of the room into the lobby, followed closely by Jackie. I glanced around, looking for Nick, but he was nowhere to be seen.

"I'm not done with you," growled Jackie, taking my elbow and holding me back.

I turned to face her, jerking my elbow out of her grasp. She stood very close to me. She was a few inches shorter than me, but her proximity was as uncomfortable as if she were at eye level.

"Oh, I think we've said everything we need to say, Jackie."

"You'll want to hear this. I don't know what it is you think you know but let me make something very clear to you. Don't even think about revealing confidential Verigro documents or corporate secrets. If you do, it will be the worst career move you've ever made in your life. Do we understand each other?"

"Can you say that a little louder," I said, reaching into my pocket and pulling out my phone. "I'm not certain that I got all that."

"What are you doing?" Jackie stepped backward.

"I'm recording you. I'm a reporter, after all. Now, I believe you were in the process of threatening my job and quite possibly my life. What exactly did you mean by that?"

"No comment," she said, and continued to step back. Jackie turned and began walking briskly down the corridor. She went around the corner and was gone.

I smiled. Sometimes it's good to be a member of the press.

I looked around. No one was paying me any attention. Peter's door was twenty feet away. I casually made my way over there and rested my hand on the door handle. Before I could open it, that same nurse came forward. Shit.

"What do you think you're doing?" he demanded.

"I just want to say goodbye to Peter," I lied.

"And I told you, no more visitors. It's time to go."

"But I…" I began.

"Please don't make me call security," he said. He looked like he meant it.

"All right. When are visiting hours?"

"Tomorrow," he said, pointedly.

"Fine," I said. I headed toward the elevators.

I pulled my phone out of my pocket and dialed Nick. Nothing happened. I glanced at the phone and noticed that there was no signal in the hospital. Shit again.

Our rendezvous plan was to meet at the car in the parking structure. Hopefully he was waiting at the car.

I stepped onto the elevator and considered what to do next. I couldn't leave Peter in the hospital, not overnight. If Jackie could get one henchman, she could get an army. I'd scared her away for the moment, but she would be back, and I still needed Peter to make this story work.

The elevator doors opened, and I walked to the entrance to the parking garage. It took me a few minutes to get there. I hoped Nick would have an idea, because I was starting to run out.

I arrived at the stolen car and looked inside. Two men sat inside.

I almost ran. It would have been the sensible thing to do. But my curiosity got the better of me. I bent down and took a better look at them.

One was Nick. The other was Peter.

"Get in," Nick said, "we don't have much time."

I hopped into the passenger seat, and Nick pulled out of the spot.

"Peter!" I exclaimed. "How the hell did you get here?"

"Nick came and got me after you got rid of Jackie," he said softly. He was clutching his stomach, and I could see bandages where the tubes used to go in.

"Are you all right?"

"He will be," Nick said. "I think."

"Did you tell him what happened?"

"Not yet," Nick said. He had driven out of the parking lot and was turning onto the street. "Now that we've got him, where are we going?"

"Somewhere safe."

Nick snorted. "Where's that?"

I smiled. "I'll tell you when we get there."

Chapter Twenty-One

"What did Errol say?" asked Nick as I hung up the phone.

"He says he knows a place between here and Chicago where we can meet him. It's out of the way. It's safe."

"It better be," Peter said. "So far, you and your network have been doing an amazingly shitty job of protecting me."

I turned in my seat to glare at him. "You haven't exactly been forthcoming with information though, have you?"

Peter looked out the window. "I told you everything you needed to know."

"Oh really? How about this one: Why don't you explain why a background check on you comes up empty before about five years ago?"

"I…" he stammered.

"Well?" I prompted.

"I may have served some time in prison," he said.

Nick turned his head to look at Peter. "You may have?"

"All right, I did."

I sighed. Now we were getting somewhere. "What were you in for?"

"I…" he stammered again. "I stole some priceless artifacts from Iran."

"I knew it!" I shouted. "I knew you had to have been in the military. That's how you know Warren, isn't it?"

Peter looked at me, surprised. He hesitated, and I guessed he was trying to phrase his answer. "Warren did me a favor once. A big favor."

"Such as?" I prompted.

"I'd rather not say," he replied. He looked away, out the window, at the nearly non-existent scenery.

My reporter's curiosity kicked in. I didn't like unanswered questions. "You served together, didn't you?"

"Something like that," he said.

"Peter," I said sternly, "we can't help you unless you tell us the truth. Your evasions aren't helping at all."

"I've told you the truth. I told you everything you need to know about BioStar to bring down Verigro. Isn't that enough?"

"No," I replied. "I'm a big picture person. If I don't know everything there is to know about a story, I can't tell the story the way it needs to be told. I miss critical points, and I get in trouble. I don't know what you're thinking about this process, but even if we blow the whistle on Verigro, Jackie is going to fight this. She's going to claim that you made it up, that you are responsible, that you were keeping the truth from her, that you don't know what you are talking about. Verigro isn't just going to collapse under the weight of your allegations. Telling this story is the beginning, not the end."

"I know all that. But if you knew what I know, you'd see that there's no way Jackie can weasel her way out of this one."

"Damn it, Peter. I want to know what you know. What do I have to do to get you to trust me?"

"Publish this story. Get it to the public, before anyone else dies from it, before any more lives are ruined."

"Is that why you're doing this? To protect people?"

"Of course. Why else?"

I huffed. "I don't know. You tell me."

Peter paused. He seemed frustrated. I didn't know if it was because he wanted to tell me what was going on and felt he couldn't, or because he wanted me to stop asking questions. Either way, I could see that he was shutting down. Pushing him wasn't going to help. I had to let him tell the story at his own pace. I thought he had given me a full interview that first night two days ago, but evidently there was more to this than he was letting on. Peter had a lot to lose—including his life—by coming forward. And until I had the full story, especially the documentation that Peter had promised me, I couldn't afford to piss him off. Not yet.

"Did you get it?" Peter asked after a long time.

I turned in my seat to look at him. "Get what?"

"Marvin," he said.

"Right here," I said, holding the decapitated figurine. "It's a memory chip, right?"

"No."

"No?" asked Nick from the driver's seat.

"If it isn't, what is it?" I asked.

Peter shook his head. "It's a key. A decryption key."

That brought me up short. "You're kidding. That's what Godzilla was looking for?"

"Yes," Peter said simply.

I had to bite my tongue before I took his head off for playing with my life. "Okay," I said instead, "what's it decrypt?"

"The Verigro database. All the documentation you could ever want on the connection between BioStar and WBS is accessible with that thing."

I stared at him a long time. "Why didn't you show that to us earlier?"

"You didn't ask," he replied. "Besides, if 'Godzilla,' as you call him, had found it, we'd all be dead right now."

I shuddered to think about that. I had been in some scary positions before, but I couldn't remember being that scared any time in recent memory. The thought of that guy filleting me….

I shook my head to rid myself of the image. "How does it work?" I asked as I shrugged off the fear. "The key, I mean."

"It works over the internet. Verigro uses keys in addition to usernames and passwords to access its systems. It's like using your ATM card. You have to have something and know something to get in. We find it seriously improves the security of our systems."

I nodded. "Well, obviously someone knows you have it. Can't they just delete your access from their system and leave us in the cold?"

Peter smiled. "Not this one. Sure, they could delete the entire database and start over from scratch, but that would cost hundreds of million dollars and bring Verigro's operations crashing to a halt for months, costing them close to a billion dollars. I seriously doubt that Jackie would take that step. And they can't just delete my accounts. It won't do them any good. Marvin there accesses the master account which allows me to get to any part of the database. It's my own little back door. I installed it myself as soon as I became Chief Operating Officer. Believe me, they'd be shooting themselves in the foot if they tried to lock me out."

"Well, you better hope that someone didn't catch on to your little trick," I said, "or we're all screwed."

"They hadn't figured it out as of two days ago," he smirked. "Something tells me that they won't catch on before we get what we want."

I turned around to look out the front window. I watched the cars dancing ballet with us. Then something occurred to me. "Why can't they just delete the reports? Wouldn't that put a crimp in your style?"

"Because I made duplicates of everything," he said. "Don't worry, Charlotte. Everything is going to be fine."

I scoffed. "That's easy for you to say."

Chapter Twenty-Two

"Is this the right place?" I asked. Nick had brought the car to a stop in front of a large industrial building or warehouse or something. The painted metal walls were rusting, and what was left of a sign hung sideways near the roof. Graffiti covered every available surface.

The warehouse was in a little town just across the Wisconsin-Illinois border called Bannockburn. None of us had ever heard of it.

"According to the GPS it is," replied Nick. He opened the door and stepped out of the car. "Are you certain Errol understood you?"

"You heard me on the phone with him," I insisted. I got out of the car too. I stood and looked toward one end of the road in front of the building, then to the other. "Maybe he's just being cautious."

"I don't like it," Peter said through the open window. "The place is deserted. We're at least half a mile from the next human being. If something happened here, no one would ever know it." He sniffed the air. "It feels like an ambush."

I had to agree with him, but if I believed Peter, I would have to believe that Errol was setting us up, which made even less sense. Errol was one of the good guys. I pulled my phone from my pocket and checked the time. "We're early. They'll probably be here in a few minutes. Let's go inside."

Nick came around the front of the car. "I'm with Peter. This isn't right."

"What are you two saying? That Errol wants us dead? That simply doesn't work for me."

Peter stayed in the car. "Are you willing to risk your life over your trust for Errol? Because I'm not."

"Why? What do you know that I don't?"

Peter remained silent. He kept searching the rooftops for something to be scared of.

I approached his window and bent down to get close to his face. "Peter, if there ever was a time to tell the complete story, now would be it. What is it that scares you?"

"I told you. It doesn't feel right."

"I'm sorry, Peter, but if you are asking me to trust your gut over mine, I choose mine."

I headed toward the door, a sliding metal contraption that sat a quarter of the way open. I put my shoulder behind it and shoved the door the rest of the way open and looked back at Nick and Peter. They were still at the car, looking worried.

"What's it going to be?" I asked them.

Peter opened the back door and stepped cautiously out of the car. He and Nick walked forward, carefully scanning the rooftops. I waited until they were at the door, and then headed inside.

The interior was lit by skylights, most of which were smashed out, and a few other open doors. The graffiti inside made the walls outside seem like a child's finger painting. The images were large, elaborate, and colorful. It had taken someone a long time to tag all this. Obviously, the warehouse had been out of business for quite a while.

Boxes, tools, and equipment littered the floor, making it more of a maze than an open space. Some of the boxes were six feet high, made of metal, and covered in multicolored paint and a thick layer of dust, which rose in clouds in the streaming daylight.

The dust made me sneeze once, then twice. I almost didn't hear the gun slide being pulled back.

I spun around, searching for the source of the sound. Nick stood a few feet away, pistol in hand.

"What the fuck are you doing?" I demanded. "Where did you get that?"

He pointed the gun toward the floor. "I got it from that guy who tried to kill us back at Peter's house. Remember him? Besides, I'm just being cautious. If Errol's people are nice to us, they won't ever need to know it's here."

"Put that damned thing away," I insisted. "If Errol's people are as nervous as we are, just carrying that thing is a good way to get shot."

A shadow moved across the wall, and Peter's head snapped around. "What was that?"

"Hello?" called a voice from the other side of the warehouse. "Anyone here?"

Instantly I began to feel that this was a bad idea after all.

"Ms. Wilson?" called a woman's voice.

My mouth was dry, and I swallowed. Here we go. "Yes, we're back here."

"Have you got Mr. Youngs with you?" She came closer. She had dark hair, stood a little shorter than me, and she walked quickly toward us. She was accompanied by a man, tall, slender, serious. They seemed familiar.

"He's here too."

"Excellent," said the woman. "We wouldn't want to leave him behind." The woman looked at me, and I recognized her immediately.

"Donna?" I asked.

"That's Detective Sergeant Lewis to you."

I couldn't figure it out. "What are you doing here? This isn't Milwaukee."

"Why, no, it isn't," said the man. Detective Simpson, the cop from Milwaukee. "You were ordered not to cross the state line just a few hours ago. That's grounds to arrest you right there."

"Yeah, but you're a bit out of your jurisdiction, aren't you?" replied Nick.

"Well," said Simpson, "we could probably make it work by claiming hot pursuit." He took his badge off his belt and placed it in his coat pocket. "Or we could dispense with the formalities."

"What's going on?" I asked.

Detective Simpson sneered at me. "What's going on is you're in the wrong place at the wrong time."

Donna smiled. "We're not here to arrest you." She put her hand on her pistol.

"Don't move," Nick said, drawing his gun. It caught on his clothes, and he couldn't bring it up.

"Weapon!" cried Detective Simpson, shooting as he drew.

I dove to the left. Peter dove to the right. And Nick went over backwards, a hole in his chest the size of a basketball.

"Nick!" I screamed from behind a large, graffiti-covered metal box.

"Get her," Donna ordered.

"Right," said Simpson.

I scrambled around the far side of the box. A box of tools sat on the floor. A crowbar stuck out from it. It was my only shot. I picked up the crowbar and hid behind the corner of the box.

I waited. My blood pumped in my ears, and I could barely breathe. If I didn't do this right, if I didn't get him in one shot, then....

Simpson's head came around the corner. I almost forgot to swing. The crowbar came around, claw first, and caught Simpson in the temple. He screamed. His gun fired as he went down. The bullet caught me in the arm, and I fell. I hit my head on something hard, and I could barely see from the pain. I grasped my head and tried not to cry out.

"Bill?" called Donna. "Bill, report."

Oh, God. She's going to find me. She's going to find me and kill me like they killed Nick.

"Bill, answer me!"

I was dizzy, and my left arm didn't want to work. I saw Simpson on the ground with the crowbar embedded in his head. His gun lay on the ground next to his hand.

Some part of my brain that still functioned shouted at me to get the gun. Apparently, I had enough sense to listen to that voice, because I went over and put my hand on it.

"Freeze," screamed Donna, who I found standing above me. "Toss the gun," she ordered. "Toss it."

I threw the gun. I could hear it land some distance away. I concentrated on not dying.

She was sweating, upset. "I can't decide what to do with you: kill you or haul you in for killing my partner."

I was terrified, but my professional curiosity got the better of me. "Why are you doing this?" I asked.

"You're a thorn in Jackie Hughes's side."

"And what are you? The janitor, cleaning up Hughes's messes?"

"Thanks for helping me decide whether to kill you," she said, and took aim at my head.

I closed my eyes.

The BOOM of the gun was tremendous. I flinched, expecting to cease to exist. But I didn't cease.

I opened my eyes again. Donna lay on the ground, not far from Simpson. The side of her head was missing.

Peter stood over her, Nick's pistol smoking in one hand, the other clutching his bleeding side.

"Are you all right?" he asked. He was breathing hard.

"I don't think so." I stood unsteadily and examined the carnage around me.

Simpson. Donna. And Nick.

"Nick," I said softly. I knew it wouldn't do me any good, but there was the slightest bit of comfort in saying his name. I began to stagger over to where he lay. I couldn't get it into my mind that he was really gone.

"We have to get out of here. Now!" insisted Peter.

"But what about…" I began, gesturing at Nick.

"Leave him. Come on, we have to go." He handed me the Glock, and then he fished through Nick's pockets for the keys. He stood and shouted, "Move!"

Walking was like moving through molten lead. Everything around me was red, and my feet felt like they were melted to the floor.

Peter took me by my good arm and began dragging me toward the car. The blinding sunlight seared my eyes.

"No one's in sight," Peter said. "Here, you drive."

"I can't drive," I said. "My arm doesn't work."

"I'm less worried about your arm than your head. Your pupils are different sizes. You have a concussion. Give me the keys and help me into the driver's seat."

I handed them to him. He put his arm around me and together we staggered around to the driver's side of the car. His gut must have been hurting him something terrible, but he only groaned when he sat. I closed his door, using the car as a crutch, made my way around to the other side. I got in the passenger side as best I could. I dreaded putting on my seatbelt.

Peter started the car and drove out onto the road. He drove at a pace so slow I thought we would be pulled over for obstructing traffic.

I looked at my arm. It wasn't bleeding very badly. My head, on the other hand, was another story.

"Where are we going?" I asked after a while.

"We'll figure that out on the road. Right now, we have to stop your bleeding."

"You're bleeding too," I observed.

"It's not bad," he winced. After a few moments, we spotted a gas station, and he pulled over and parked next to the restrooms. He went inside and came out with two large handfuls of paper towels.

"These will have to do," he said. Peter gave me a wad of towels and clapped them over the cut on my head. "Hold this here," he said, "and I'll look at your arm."

"What about you?" I asked lamely.

"That's my problem," he said. "Right now, you have two jobs: stop bleeding and stay awake. Got it? No passing out."

"No passing out," I repeated.

A police car drove by, more slowly than either of us would have liked.

"We have to get out of here," he said.

"Uh-huh," I said weakly. There wasn't much more I could say.

The police cruiser drove on, and Peter started the car. He turned on the radio as loud as it would go.

"God! Turn that off!" I cried.

"Not until I'm sure you're in the clear," he shouted over the noise.

With as much strength as I could muster, I said, "I'm fine, Peter. Just drive."

He looked at me for a long moment. Then, clutching a wad of towels to his gut, he pulled out of the gas station.

It was the last thing I remembered.

Chapter Twenty-Three

I woke up to see Peter standing over me. I was lying in a lumpy bed, covered to the shoulders with a dingy blanket. I looked around where we were—it appeared to be a small motel room. My arm was taped up and hurt like hell, but not as much as my head.

"What happened?"

Peter glared at me without much sympathy. "Didn't I tell you not to pass out?" he growled.

"I…. Yeah, I think you did. Sorry," I offered.

Peter stepped away from me and over to the bureau. He was bent over, and his skin was pale and damp. "I got your bleeding stopped. You should have some food. I ordered pizza—they were the only ones that delivered around here. Are you hungry?"

I thought about it for a long time. "I think so?" I said.

"Okay. Help yourself."

Peter had managed to bandage his mid-section—it appeared to be a pretty good job. I sat up and instantly regretted it. My headache got much worse, and my arm throbbed with pain.

Only after that did I notice that I wasn't wearing a shirt or a bra.

I pulled the covers over myself.

"Where's my blouse?" I demanded.

Peter didn't look up. I got the impression he was watching me in the mirror. "It was soaked in blood, so I threw it out. There's a clean t-shirt for you on the bedside table."

"Did you have to take my bra off too?" I accused him as I reached over and pulled the t-shirt toward me. I pulled it over my head, leaving my injured arm inside.

This time, he did turn around. "I'm sorry if I embarrassed you. I couldn't get the bandage over your arm with your bra still on. I figured saving your life was more important than your modesty." He didn't wait for me to respond. Instead he went to the small table and put a piece of pizza on a paper plate. He handed it to me. "We need to hole up somewhere. Somewhere safe. Somewhere with a doctor."

"Where are we?" I asked.

He served himself a piece of pizza. "Just outside Rockford."

"Where's Rockford?"

"Due west of where we were ambushed," he said, matter-of-factly.

A thought occurred to me. I wanted to dismiss it, but it was our only option. "I know a place," I said. "It's a long way from here."

Peter chewed his pizza. He swallowed and said, "How far?"

"I'd guess twelve or thirteen hundred miles."

Peter considered that. "That's about fifteen or twenty hours of driving, especially if we're going to keep from being pulled over. We'll have to ditch the Mercedes."

"Do you think we can get another car?" I asked.

"I saw a used car lot a few miles back. I checked your bag. Between us we have about fifteen hundred dollars in cash. We could get a car."

"You went through my bag?"

Peter shrugged.

"Okay." I checked the calendar on my phone. It was still Friday, which meant Samarie's phone would be on. I dialed.

"Who are you calling?" Peter demanded.

"My daughter," I whispered.

"Are you sure that's a good idea?"

I ignored him.

"Mommy?" Samarie's sweet voice came on just before the fourth ring. "I thought you forgot about me."

"Hi, Pumpkin. Of course I wouldn't forget about you. I've been looking forward to calling you all week. I've got good news for you. I'll be seeing you sooner than I thought. Maybe tomorrow."

"Yay! Daddy, Mom's coming here! Tomorrow!"

I could hear Warren, normally a very quiet man, say in the background, "She is?"

"Listen, sweetie, could I speak to your father? It's kind of important."

"Daddy, Mom wants to talk to you!" screamed Samarie. I had the image in my head that Warren was standing right next to her, knowing full well that she would have screamed anyway.

"Lotte? What's going on?" Warren's voice was full of concern.

"Do you have a doctor there? Not a veterinarian, but a people doctor?"

"Why?" demanded Warren.

"Look, do you or don't you?"

"Yes. We have a pretty good one. Are you hurt?"

I sighed again. "Warren, I need somewhere to hole up for a while."

"Lotte, what's going on?" he repeated.

I hesitated. "Remember that story I was working on? Well, it's kind of gone sideways on me. Can you put me up?"

"What does 'sideways' mean? What have you gotten yourself into?"

"I can't explain right now. Can you put us up or not?"

"Wait a second. A minute ago, you said 'me.' Now it's 'us.' Who are you bringing with you?"

"An old friend of yours. Peter Youngs."

"Who?" he demanded.

"Warren, please. I don't have the energy to argue with you. I'm going to be there tomorrow, probably late. As soon as possible, at any rate. I really need your help. Can you do that for me?"

Warren huffed. "All right. Fine. I'll leave Samarie's phone on, and I'll have Patricia standing by."

"Patricia? Why her?"

"She's our doctor," Warren said simply.

"Of course she is. All right. See you tomorrow." I hung up before he could say anything else.

"You called Warren?" asked Peter. "I thought you were calling your daughter."

"Trust me," I said, "this is our only option."

Peter nodded. He finished his slice of pizza, stood, and limped into the bathroom. I began eating my slice. A moment later, he came out and sat down on the other side of the bed. That was when I realized there was only one bed in the room.

"Uh," I began.

"Charlotte, I'm flattered," he said, "but even if I wanted to try something funny, I'm too hurt and tired to even consider it. So get over yourself. I'm going to sleep." He reached over and turned off the lamp on his side of the bed. In a few minutes, he was breathing deeply and evenly.

I thought about sleeping on the floor, but with my arm and head injured like that, I dismissed that idea quickly. Peter obviously had no plans to make a pass at me. It took me another five seconds to realize I was being silly.

I finished my pizza, used the bathroom, and got into bed. I was too tired to care whether he was there or not. I laid down and switched off the lamp. I was asleep before my head hit the pillow.

Chapter Twenty-Four

It was late Sunday, not Saturday, when we arrived at the Orchard, much later than we expected. Between the two of us, there was no way we could make it in one run, so we had stopped over in Rapid City, which cost us most of a day. My arm and head were healing acceptably, but Peter's gut wound wouldn't stop bleeding. There were several points where we discussed taking him to a hospital, but he insisted he could make it all the way to Bozeman.

Peter was pale and sweating when I got out of the car to open the gate. I prayed that I could still remember the code. After three tries, I realized the combination was Samarie's birthday. The chain came apart in my hand, and I pushed the gate open with all the strength I had left.

The winding road was painful for both of us. The way Peter looked, I'm surprised he could drive at all. I checked the clock on the dash. It was eight-thirty, just after sunset. It would be dark when we arrived.

I directed Peter to pull up next to the infirmary. Warren and a few more people came around the corner. One or two had shotguns. "Put your hands on the wheel where they can see them," I told Peter. He did as he was told.

Warren approached my window. "Are you all right?"

"Not really. Is Patricia ready?"

"Depends on how bad it is." Warren looked through the window and shined a flashlight on me. "What happened to you?" Then Peter turned to face him, and Warren brought up his lamp. "Jesus," Warren eyed the bloody bandage. "What's going on here, Lotte?"

"We were in a scuffle."

"A scuffle?" Warren repeated.

"I'll explain later. Come on, let's get him inside."

Two men helped Peter out of the car and walked him into the infirmary where Patricia was waiting.

"Where's Samarie?" I asked.

Warren grimaced. "She's with Paige's family. It took all my authority to keep her from flopping all over you when you got here."

"Get him up on the table," Patricia instructed. The two men picked Peter up and laid him down gently on the padded table. She had them pull his shirt off and then she peeled the bandage back. "What happened to him?"

"He was stabbed about three days ago. We had to get him out of the hospital early. Can you help him?"

"A hospital is exactly where he should be!"

"No," Peter said. His voice was stronger than I expected it to be. "No one can know I'm here."

"Why not?" asked Warren.

"It's a long story," I said, dismissively.

"Make it short," replied Warren.

"Can you two talk about this outside?" Patricia said. It was an order, not a question.

Warren nodded his head to the side, directing me out of the room. I followed him out.

"What the hell is going on? What are you doing here with that guy?"

"You know him?" I asked.

Warren hesitated. "Yes. At least, I did. I'm not surprised to see him wounded. But how did you get mixed up with him?"

"He's the story I've been working on. It's big, Warren, really big. People will kill over this story." Nick suddenly popped into my mind. "They already have."

"And you brought this to my doorstep? What the hell is the matter with you?"

"Warren, please. I haven't asked you for a favor in years."

"You haven't? What about keeping Samarie for you?"

"You don't want her?"

"That's not the point, Lotte. We live in peace here. The whole point of the Orchard is to get away from the stresses and problems of the world out there. Now you've brought it all with you, and I don't want it here!"

"What are you going to do, turn us out?"

Warren grumbled and eyed the bandages on my arm and head.

"Come on, Warren. At least let us stay until we get better. If he's a friend of yours, you owe him at least that."

"I never said he was a friend."

"Then I'm begging you. Let us stay. Please."

Warren grumbled again. Finally he said, "Just until you're better."

"Thank you, Warren. You won't regret this."

"I already do." Warren looked me over. "We should get you inside. You don't look much better than he does."

"I can wait until Patricia is done helping Peter."

Warren sighed. "Lotte, what really happened to you?"

"It's been a long couple of days," I said to him. "I promise I'll explain later. Right now, I just want to rest."

"Your cottage is just the way you left it," he said.

"Thanks," I said. "Do me a favor and call me when Patricia is done with Peter."

"I'll do you one better. I'll send Patricia over to you. Go lie down. You look like shit."

I smiled. "You always were a charmer," I told him.

Chapter Twenty-Five

Peter slept. He slept for four days, waking only long enough to drink some water and get a little soup down. Patricia stayed by his side most of the time. She wouldn't let me anywhere near him. I got the impression she didn't like me.

I returned the sentiment. She was snooty, aloof, and sometimes downright rude. She shared Warren's opinion that we were bringing trouble to her little corner of paradise, and she didn't appreciate me being there one bit. I suppose I would have felt the same way, if I were in her shoes, but she never stopped to think about what brought us to this point. She just bitched and moaned about the trouble we were causing.

However, she was able to fix my arm. The bullet had gone straight through the flesh, missing the bone and any arteries. Patricia informed me coldly that if the bullet had been two inches to the right, I would have bled out in a matter of minutes. She almost seemed disappointed that I hadn't. So much for her bedside manner.

I spent my time either by sleeping or with Samarie. After Samarie decided I wasn't going to die, she became bored with me, and she would run off to play with her friend Paige as soon as it was polite to do so.

I tried calling George about seven times over those four days, but each time, I got the same response. "Agent Martinez is out in the field."

I also spent a lot of time thinking about Nick, especially at night when Samarie was asleep and there was no one else around. I had believed Errol when he said we'd be safe. Nick and Peter had wanted to leave, and I talked them into staying. Peter tried to convince me on the ride to the Orchard that if Nick hadn't pulled a gun on two trained police officers, he wouldn't have been killed. But I couldn't help but think that the whole thing was my fault. In fact, if Detective Donna hadn't confessed she was working for Jackie Hughes, I'd have serious doubts about Errol right about then.

On the afternoon of the third day, Warren knocked on the door to my cottage. I bade him enter.

"Patricia says he's going to make it," he said by way of greeting.

"Thank God," I said.

"Are you going to explain to me what this story is about?" he asked.

"Are you going to explain to me how you know Peter?" I replied.

That brought Warren up short.

Before he could say anything, I continued, "Come on, Warren. You know full well that I'm not going to let it go until you tell me."

"I knew McCormick in the Army. All right?" Warren said, sitting on the sofa next to me.

"Who's McCormick?"

"I don't understand. Peter McCormick. That's his name."

I couldn't help myself. I laughed. "Of course. That explains a lot. No wonder we couldn't figure out where he was before five years ago!"

"You don't even know his name?" demanded Warren.

"Well, I do. Or I did. He calls himself Peter Youngs now."

"Really? I suppose that's not too surprising. I probably would have changed my identity too."

I frowned. "What the hell is that supposed to mean?"

Warren paused. I could see the wheels turning in his head. "Maybe I should let him tell you."

"Why don't you tell me the basics, and I'll get the specifics from him."

"Fine," he said, exasperated. "Fine. I'll tell you. I can see that it's the only way I can get you to drop it."

"You know it," I smiled.

"Peter McCormick was a captain under my command."

"I don't remember meeting him when I was embedded with you," I said.

"He commanded a different company. Are you going to let me tell this story?"

"Sorry."

"McCormick was a good man and a good soldier. He saved my ass on a couple of occasions. He was a cool thinker, very sure of himself. Intelligent. Made the right decisions at the right time. I even recommended that he be promoted. That is, until...."

I waited this time. When it was pretty clear that Warren was stuck, I prompted him with, "Until what?"

"Until he attempted to smuggle ancient artifacts out of Iran. Stole them right out of a local museum. He and three other soldiers, two sergeants and a corporal. Thought they could smuggle them out in a coffin. Naturally, they got caught."

"Yeah, that's pretty much what he told me." I paused, confused. "What's that got to do with you?" I asked.

"Since I was his brigade commander at the time, the son of a bitch got me court-martialed. I was lucky enough to be exonerated. But McCormick and his two accomplices were sentenced to ten years. He appealed to me. Asked me to intervene on his behalf. Said I owed him, and I suppose I did. So I pulled a few strings and got his sentence reduced to six years. So we're even."

I heard everything he said, but I got stuck on one thing, and I could feel my temper rising because of it. "You were court-martialed? When were you going to tell me this? Wasn't that right after we got married?"

"Yeah, we were married," he sighed. "I didn't tell you because you were worried enough about me as it was.

With you back in the States taking care of Samarie, there wasn't anything you could do about it anyway. I figured if it became a problem, I would tell you."

"You thought being court-martialed wasn't a problem?" I was exasperated. "What the hell else weren't you telling me about back then?"

"Nothing you need to know now, that's for sure."

I stood up, began pacing. "We were married. We had a child. And you didn't have the courtesy to tell me that you almost went to federal prison? What the fuck is wrong with you?"

"You see? You just can't resist arguing with me, can you?"

"Why you smug, self-centered, arrogant, lying bastard. I can't believe you think that it was okay to keep being court-martialed from me. This is exactly the kind of macho horseshit that made me divorce you."

Warren furrowed his brow. "I thought we got divorced because you didn't want to live here with me at the Orchard," he said quietly.

"Maybe that was part of it. I never understood why you quit your career in the Army to start this… this funny farm. You never even consulted me, never asked me if I wanted to give up my career as a journalist so that you could look after your little crackpot buddies. And now I see why. You were never honest with me."

"I was honest when I said I loved you," Warren said softly.

I laughed. "Well, isn't that a pretty sentiment. If you really loved me, you could have at least been up front with me. I could have forgiven you your failings, Warren. What I can't forgive are the lies."

"Which is why I live here, and you live… out there," he said, gesturing vaguely to the rest of the universe.

"What about Patricia? Do you tell her everything you lied to me about?"

It was Warren's turn to stand. "Lotte, leave Patricia out of this."

"I'm going to take that for a 'no.' Maybe I should have a little heart-to-heart with her and let her know what she's getting herself into."

Warren took a step towards me. Not enough to get in my personal space, but enough to be menacing. "Now you listen to me. You are my guest here. And you're hiding from someone. The authorities, perhaps. Maybe some more of McCormick's criminal buddies. I don't know, and I don't want to know. But if you want me to 'aid and abet' you two, I suggest you keep your opinions to yourself. Do you read me?"

"Are you actually threatening me?" I asked. I was surprised. Warren didn't make idle threats.

"It's not a threat, Lotte, it's a promise. There's a Sheriff's station not ten miles from here. I'm guessing you don't want a visit from him. So don't push it. Copy?"

I looked at Warren for a long time. Neither of us spoke. Finally, I lowered my eyes. "Roger that," I said.

"Good." Warren headed for the front door. Without another word, he stormed through and slammed the screen behind him.

I stared at the door a long time. "Fuck," I said.

Chapter Twenty-Six

"Agent Martinez," George said. I breathed a sigh of relief. I had begun to wonder if I would ever reach him.

"George," I said, pacing my small front room. "It's Charlie. I need your help. I'm in deep shit."

"Charlie?" George shouted. Then he lowered his voice. "Where are you? Do you have any idea how many people are looking for you?"

"No, but I can guess. And I'd bet there's even more people on the other side of the fence who'd love to find me as well."

"You killed two police officers," he whispered. "That's a federal offense, Charlie."

"It was self-defense, George. They were going to kill us. They shot Nick in cold blood."

In a low voice, George said, "Self-defense against a police officer is a hard case to make. You'd have to prove that they were acting in a criminal manner. I don't think even you can talk your way out of this one."

"Think about it, George. Did anyone stop to ask themselves what two detectives from Milwaukee were doing in a warehouse in Nowheresville, Illinois?" Before George could respond, I continued. "I'll bet you a dollar that you found Simpson's badge in his right coat pocket, and only his fingerprints on it. You want to know why? Because he put it away right before he shot Nick." I could feel the tears welling up in my voice. "If we hadn't defended ourselves, they would have murdered me and Peter on Jackie Hughes's orders."

"Charlie, I want to believe you, I want to help you, but this is too much. You actually want me to believe that Jackie Hughes, the CEO of one of the largest corporations in America and a candidate for U.S. Senate, is behind all this? And that she had veteran cops on her payroll, ready to carry out her orders to kill you? No one is going to believe that. Certainly not a jury."

I stopped pacing. "George, listen to me. Something big is going on. Remember how I asked you to track down Peter Youngs? I know why you didn't find anything. His name is Peter McCormick. He was in federal prison for six years—right before he started working for Verigro. Three years later, he became their COO. Something screwy is going on in that company."

"Charlie…" George said with warning in his voice.

"There's more. I'm following a story. A story Jackie Hughes wants covered up. BioStar is killing people. Thousands of people, maybe millions. And if my information is correct, Jackie has known about it for years. Peter tried to get the story to me, and that's why they attacked us. I'm on the verge of proving it. I just need a little more time."

I could tell George was losing his patience. "Time to do what?"

"If I can prove that BioStar is causing Witko-Byrne, I can prove that Peter and I are innocent of everything we're being accused of."

"Peter Youngs is supposed to be in a hospital. You kidnapped him. Those detectives were in pursuit of you when you gunned them down." He paused. "That's the official story, anyway."

"Yeah, well, the official story is a complete fabrication. Has anyone been back to Peter's house in the last forty-eight hours?"

"Not as far as I know. Why? What are we going to find?"

"Either a lot of blood and teeth, or a dead body missing them."

There was a long pause. I guessed that George was trying to assimilate what I was saying.

"You..." he choked a bit. "You killed someone else? They have a word for what you're doing, Charlie. It's called spree killing."

"You have to believe me. He was going to kill us, George. Nick and me. So Nick tripped him down the stairs."

"Where are you?" demanded George. "I can't protect you if you're running around Hell's half-acre kidnapping witnesses and killing cops."

"Don't change the subject. Look, send someone to Peter's house—someone not on the Milwaukee police force. If Toothless is still there, check his phone. You should find a record of a direct-connect. Trace it. Whoever was on the other end is the person who's behind all this. And I'll bet you it leads back to Jackie Hughes."

"Are you listening to yourself? You're making wild accusation after wild accusation. Even I'm having trouble believing you. If someone catches you, I can't protect you."

"I can't come in, George. Not yet. There are too many people I can't trust. Errol Foster may be one of them."

"Now you're accusing Foster? This is too much. Come on, Charlie. Turn yourself in. It's the only way."

"Not yet," I repeated. "Soon. Just give me a little more time."

"When, then?" demanded George.

"A week. Two at the most. By then I should be able to wrap this up with a bow for you."

"No. I can't do it," George said.

I turned and saw Samarie and Paige looking in the window. They both ducked down as soon as I spotted them.

"George, I have to go. I'll call you when I can."

"No, Charlie, wait!"

"Goodbye, George." I disconnected. I slipped the phone into my pocket and headed for the door. "Samantha Marie Boyd," I called. I hoped using her full name would have the effect I wanted—instilling infinite dread in her little heart. "Get your behind in here."

Samarie came around the corner, slowly, guiltily. Paige was nowhere to be seen.

"Come here, young lady," I said in my best "angry mother" voice.

Samarie walked toward me reluctantly. I could see by the look on her face that she'd rather be anywhere on the surface of the planet, but she knew that running from me wouldn't help.

"Inside," I ordered, holding the door open. I followed her into the front room. "Sit," I commanded. She sat.

"Mom, I…" she began.

"What did you hear?" I demanded.

"Nothing!" she insisted.

"Are you sure you want to start off this conversation with a lie?" I folded my arms.

"I only heard the last little bit, I swear!" She crossed her heart. I tried not to smile at the childish gesture.

"Do you understand how wrong it is to eavesdrop?" I asked sternly.

"I'm sorry, Mom. I thought you were yelling at Daddy again."

"What do you mean, again?" I asked, surprised.

"Like you did yesterday. Please don't yell anymore, Mom."

"You were listening then too?" I put my hand on my head. "Samarie, what in the world is wrong with you? Since when do you listen in on other people's conversations? I didn't raise you to be a snoop."

"I'm sorry," she offered again.

"Samarie, sometimes grown-ups have private conversations that children shouldn't be listening to. Grown-ups are entitled to their privacy." I began pacing. "I don't want to ever catch you eavesdropping again. I don't want to hear from anyone else that you were listening in on their conversations, either. No more. Got it? You're done."

"Yes, Mom," she said obediently.

"Now, what am I going to do with you?"

"No," cried Samarie.

"I'm going to talk to your father about this. For the moment, I want you to go back to your father's house and go to your room. And stay there until someone gets you."

"Yes, Mom." She got up from the sofa and walked to the door, tears in her eyes. "Mom?" she asked.

"What?" I replied.

"You're in trouble, aren't you?"

That brought me up short. How could I answer that question? "It's nothing you need to worry about," I said finally.

"I'm scared, Mommy. I'm afraid something bad is going to happen to you."

I walked over to her and put my good arm around her. "Nothing is going to happen to me," I said to her, and for that moment I meant it. "I love you, Samarie. I promise nothing bad will happen. Okay?"

"Okay," she said.

I embraced her for a long moment. Then I held her at arm's length.

"Samarie…" I began. "I'm sorry. I may have overreacted. I won't tell your father."

"Thank you, Mommy," she beamed.

"All right. Get out of here."

She went. I could see Paige peeking around the corner of a far building. Samarie went over to her, and they ran off somewhere out of sight.

I went back to the sofa and sat.

Tears began flooding my eyes, and I found myself sobbing. I had lied to her, though I wished I had been telling the truth. I didn't want anything bad to happen to me either.

Chapter Twenty-Seven

"Patricia?" I opened the door, surprised to see her on my porch.

"May I come in?" she asked humbly.

"I… sure. Come in. *Mi casa es su casa* and all that, right? After all, the Orchard is more your home than mine."

"Thanks," she said. She came inside and sat on one of the chairs next to the sofa. Then she looked up at me expectantly.

"Oh," I said. "I guess I'm being a bad host. Can I get you something to drink? I think I have some lemonade."

"Lemonade would be nice," she replied.

I wandered off to the kitchen and poured two glasses of lemonade from a pitcher I had in the little dorm fridge. Why they didn't have full-sized refrigerators at the Orchard, I'll never know. Maybe they used up too much electricity. My guess was that they were too modern for Warren's rustic sensibilities. As it was, there was no ice for the lemonade. As a confirmed ice-chewer, I found this a bit offensive, but there was really nothing I could do about it. I wasn't planning on being at the Orchard long enough to import my own icemaker.

I watched Patricia through the doorway as I poured the lemonade. She was a little older than I had originally thought when I first saw her a week ago—she must have been about twenty-eight or thirty. She was wearing a white broomstick skirt and a loose top, which showed off her figure very much to her advantage. She was a tiny little thing—I guessed about a size two. Her face was round, tanned, pretty. If I put aside my general dislike of her, I could see something of what attracted Warren to her. Whether I liked it or not, she was lovely.

"Here you are," I said, placing the glass on the coffee table in front of her. "Now, to what do I owe the honor of your visit?" I asked, sitting on the far corner of the sofa.

"How's your arm coming along?" she asked.

"It hurts," I said casually. She had insisted that I come to the infirmary for her to check my arm every six hours since I got there, so that couldn't be the reason she was here. "What else can I do for you?"

"We…" she began. She paused, took a breath, and began again. "We got off on the wrong foot. I wanted to make that up to you, now that we're going to be…." She hesitated again, searching for the word. I let her search. "Now that we're both going to be sharing Samarie. Officially, I mean."

"You mean, now that you're going to be marrying my ex-husband and raising my daughter," I said. It came out with a great deal more hostility than I had originally intended.

"Uh, yes," she said. Uncomfortably, she sipped her lemonade. "Anyway, I thought it would be better for Samarie if we at least tried to get along."

"Okay, I'll buy that." Geez, what was the matter with me? I took a deep breath. "I mean, I'd like that." I leaned back on the sofa, trying to look relaxed. I doubted I succeeded.

There was a long, uncomfortable silence. Ordinarily, long uncomfortable silences didn't bother me—they could be very useful in drawing out information from an interviewee—but this time I felt the need to talk.

I sipped my lemonade and said, "So are you still getting married this week? Samarie wasn't very clear when I asked her."

"No, actually."

"No?" I asked, genuinely concerned.

"I'm afraid not. Before you and Peter showed up, we had scheduled it for tomorrow. Now that things have changed, we postponed it indefinitely."

"Why? What's changed?"

Patricia looked at me strangely, as if I had said something in a foreign language that she could not translate.

"Warren tells me you and Peter are in trouble. Peter's injuries were extensive. He didn't get that gut wound from bumping into a door. And that wound in your arm was clearly from a bullet. You must be here hiding from something or someone. Otherwise why would you come back so soon. It seemed like caution was the best course."

I sat forward again. "What exactly did Warren tell you?" I growled.

Patricia took a deep breath. "He told me you were chasing one of your stories, and that you get very wrapped up in yourself when you do that. He said that Peter was an ex-convict who was in federal prison for some time for theft of priceless artifacts. He told me that you were being evasive about your motives for coming here. And I believed him."

"I see," I said, clicking my tongue. I tried to control my frustration, but it didn't work. "Well, he seems to have covered everything."

"Look, Lotte, I don't want to fight with you, no matter what Warren says about your preferences to the contrary. I just want to do what's best for Samarie."

"And what's best for her?" I demanded.

"That she stay here," she said simply.

I huffed. "You've got her for a year at least. Isn't that enough for you?"

Patricia looked me in the eye. "I meant permanently."

"No. I told Warren that, and now I'm telling you. I am not giving up custody of my daughter."

"Every time she goes out there," Patricia said, waving her hand vaguely toward the outside world, "she risks getting sick. We're not totally isolated here. I hear things.

I know that Witko-Byrne Syndrome hits children harder than adults. You don't want her to catch it, do you?"

"You can't catch it," I heard myself saying. "It's not contagious."

"You don't know that," argued Patricia. "No one knows that."

"Yeah, well, I do," I said. I noticed I was gritting my teeth, and I tried to relax.

"With all due respect, Lotte, you're not a medical professional. I am. The data show that WBS is more than likely to be communicable. You and Peter could have brought it here. You could have contaminated all of us. That was a careless thing to do—selfish, even. You don't exactly have a track record for thinking about anyone but yourself. And Samarie needs someone who can think of her needs once in a while. That's why I think she should be here with us."

"You mean, with you, don't you?" I shouted, standing. "You think you could be a better mother to her than I can. Well let me tell you something, Patricia…."

At that moment, the door slammed open. Patricia and I turned to see Samarie running inside.

"Mom!" she shouted, coming into the front room.

I looked at her. She seemed scared.

"What's the matter, Pumpkin?"

"I wasn't eavesdropping!" she said. "I promise. But they were yelling and I couldn't help it."

"Who was yelling?" asked Patricia.

Samarie took a breath. "Daddy and Peter. I think they're going to punch each other."

"Where are they?" I asked before Patricia could.

"Daddy's office," Samarie said.

Both Patricia and I stood up and followed Samarie out the door and across the courtyard to Warren's office.

We could hear the yelling from thirty paces away. I couldn't make out what they were saying, but they seemed very sincere about out-shouting each other.

Patricia opened the door with a slam. "What in the world are you two fools yelling about?" she shouted. "And what are you doing out of bed?" she asked Peter.

Warren and Peter stared at us, dumbfounded.

"Well?" Patricia demanded.

"It's nothing," Warren said. "Right, Peter?"

"Give me one good reason I shouldn't tell both of them everything."

"Peter, this is my land. You're a guest here. And as long you're a guest, you'll abide by my rules. Copy that?"

"I don't take orders from you anymore, Warren. The last time I did, I wound up serving six years in prison."

"What's that supposed to mean?" asked Patricia.

"Maybe," I interjected, "we can continue this conversation another time," I said, nodding my head at Samarie.

Everyone turned to look at the eleven-year-old girl who was soaking in the sordid scene.

Peter grumbled.

Warren huffed.

Patricia said, "Peter, I'm taking you back to your room. You shouldn't be up for at least another day. You're going to reopen that wound if you aren't careful. Now move!"

Peter glared at her for a moment. Then he must have thought better about contradicting the woman who'd saved his life. He stomped out of Warren's office. Patricia took Samarie by the wrist and dragged her out as well. She gave one more dirty look to Warren and me, and left.

"Oh, to have been a fly on the wall for that conversation," I said. "Remind me to bug your office."

"Lotte, don't go there," he growled.

"You might as well tell me what you were talking about, Warren. I'm going to find out anyway. What did Peter mean when he said he was following your orders when he was sent to prison?"

Warren was torn. I wish I knew what was going on in his head right then, because his face was a seascape of trouble. "Peter and I were just discussing old times," he said finally.

I laughed a long, mirthful laugh. "That's beautiful," I chuckled. "You are the worst liar I've ever met, Warren. You're hiding something. What is it?"

"You're hiding something, too. Are you sure your secret isn't more dangerous than mine?"

"It isn't my secret. It's Peter's." I paused. Of course. It was so obvious. "And so is yours. What are you and Peter keeping secret, Warren?"

"You're treading on thin ice here, Lotte. Don't let your curiosity get the better of you. Leave this one alone."

I looked into Warren's face. In all the time I knew him, he never laid a hand on me in anger. But I would have been willing to bet that if I didn't let it go right then, he would have changed that trend, perhaps permanently.

"All right," I said, dropping my eyes. "I'll let it go."

"Smartest thing you ever did," he mumbled. "Now get out of my office."

I turned and left. I glanced back at his door as it shut behind me.

If Warren thought he could keep a story from me, he was dead wrong. I just had to find another way to come at it. I went back to my cottage to plan my next step. And I knew Peter was the place to start.

Chapter Twenty-Eight

Patricia finally let Peter out of the infirmary on the sixth day. She had been keeping him hostage there, not allowing me to visit for more than a few minutes at a time, and only under her direct supervision. I don't know what her role at the Orchard was the rest of the year, but she evidently loved playing doctor—or savior, or whatever term she used in the privacy of her own mind.

As it was, even after she declared him healthy if not healed, she still followed Peter around like a watchdog or a protective mother, helping him walk, insisting that he rest. He looked plenty healthy to me. Of course, I also knew what he was capable of even when he had a hole in his gut, and I owed my life to him.

A sprained ankle finally saved Peter's sanity and gave me a chance to talk to him alone for the first time. Samarie,

Paige, and another child, a boy named Stanley, had gone hiking in the foothills near the entrance road, and Stanley had climbed a tree attempting to show off. He leapt down from one of the upper branches and twisted his foot.

I wish I had had my phone out to snap a picture of Patricia's face when the children came back from their hike with Stanley injured like that. She actually seemed disappointed she wouldn't be able to follow Peter around. I promised her that I would take good care of him and whisked him away.

"Thank you," Peter said. He and I wandered between the buildings of the village, heading generally in the direction of the stables.

"What for?" I asked. I gave him my arm for support, but he barely put any pressure on it. I'll give Peter one thing. He's a fast healer.

"Rescuing me from my mother hen," he said.

I smiled. "You noticed it too?"

"She's a great doctor and a nice enough person when you let her poke and prod, but…" he trailed off, letting out a big sigh.

I chuckled. "For a while I thought Warren was replacing me with her," I said as we walked, "but I'm beginning to think that he is replacing his mother instead. I'm not too excited about her being Samarie's stepmother, but there's not a lot I can do about that now."

"Yeah, I heard they are getting married. Does that bother you?"

I scoffed. "Me? Not at all."

Peter gave me a sideways glance. "You're not a very good liar, you know that?"

"I'm not supposed to be," I replied. "I'm a reporter. I'm in the business of telling the truth." I hesitated. "I want to ask you something."

"Okay, shoot."

"What's the story between you and Warren? The real story." Before he could respond, I said, "I know you told me you went to prison for stealing artifacts—which is pretty reprehensible, if you ask me—and I know Warren told me that you got him court-martialed. But…"

Peter spoke over me. "Court-martialed? When was Warren court-martialed?"

"He…" I began. I knew that story had to be fabricated. "He said that because he was your commanding officer and responsible for your actions, he was court-martialed. He also said he was exonerated, and that you asked him to intervene in your sentencing. He said he was the one who got your sentence reduced to six years." I stopped in front of Peter and looked him in the eyes. "But that's a cover story, isn't it? You two are still hiding something, aren't you?"

"Uh…" attempted Peter.

I smiled. "Now who's the bad liar?"

"What I mean is… yes."

I hadn't expected him to confirm it. Carefully, I prompted him. "Yes, what?"

"Yes, Warren is hiding something. I suppose I am too." He stood up straight, as if he had just found his confidence. "But I'm done lying, Charlotte."

I dug my phone out of my pocket, and activated the voice recorder. "I'm listening."

"Hold on," Peter said, taking a step back. "Not yet."

"What happened to being done lying?" I asked.

"No, what I mean is, you shouldn't have to take my word for it. I want you to hear it from Warren." He turned around and practically sprinted back to Warren's office with me following closely behind.

Chapter Twenty-Nine

Peter burst into Warren's office. "Warren?" he called. Warren was there figuring numbers on a hand-held calculator.

"What do you want?" demanded Warren. "I thought you were supposed to be on bed rest."

"Patricia unchained my leg," he said as he sat in one of the chairs. I continued standing. "We've got to talk."

"Peter," Warren said, nodding at me, "If this is what I think it is, I already told you. We're not going to have this conversation. Understood?"

"No, I do not understand, Warren. BioStar is out there because of you and me. If we hadn't…."

Warren stood. "Shut up, Peter!"

"No," I said, "let him talk. How is this your fault, Warren?"

Warren pointed his finger at me. "Lotte, this is none of your business."

I took a step forward. "I'm making it my business," I snarled. "Peter said this is your fault. My life, and Samarie's, are in danger. Nick is dead. How can you say this is not my business?"

"Warren," interjected Peter. "It's time. Twelve years is long enough. Just tell her."

Warren started walking around the desk, approaching Peter, fists clenched. "Peter, nothing has changed. Keep your mouth shut, or I'll shut it for you."

"Keep your mouth shut about what?" Patricia said through an open window. She walked around to the front door and entered. "What are you hiding, Warren?"

"Patricia…" began Warren. He stood there, frozen in his footsteps.

"It's too late, Warren," I said. "Just tell us."

Warren supported himself on the desk like an old man and crumpled back into his chair. He covered his eyes. "You don't understand…" he started.

"Explain it to us," Patricia said.

Peter turned to Patricia and said, "Warren and I did some things in Iran we shouldn't have. We did it for Jackie Hughes, my boss, and Errol Foster, her boss," he said, indicating me. "BioStar was the direct result."

"Hold on. Errol? What's he got to do with this?" I asked. I held my phone close to my side. I didn't want to miss a word. I just wish Nick were with me to hear this. He would have loved it.

"Look, Verigro had just come out with SCS and created BioStar. Or at least, an early version of it. Jackie needed to get it to market as quickly as possible—SCS had put Verigro in debt up to its eyeballs, and she needed a way out. But human trials would take forever."

"Wait a second," I said, "I thought that the White House and FDA policies were to rubber stamp transgenic foods without rigorous testing."

"It is," Peter said. "Haley Bowen, the Secretary of Agriculture for the last four administrations, will approve nearly anything for market that has the smallest amount of transgenic material in it. But even though the process is accelerated, it isn't instantaneous. And it takes a while for market share to build. Jackie couldn't wait that long. She had to know BioStar was safe for humans within a year, not two or five like other transgenics. She needed human subjects, and she didn't want to be under the watchful eye of the FDA. And there was a war going on, so...."

"So you tested it on the Iranians?" Patricia said. Her voice was deadpan. "Is that what he's saying, Warren?"

Warren said nothing. He sat in his chair, eyes covered. It was hard to tell he was even breathing.

"So what happened then?" I prompted.

"Jackie needed a way into Iran. She wasn't a no-bid contractor—Verigro was too small to have that kind of political clout—but she knew someone who was."

"Errol Foster," I said. Suddenly things were making a lot more sense.

"Errol Foster," he confirmed.

I nodded. I knew he had something to do with this—Peter had been hinting at it since I met him—and this just confirmed it. "Okay. What did Errol do?"

"He sent a reporter—her name was Anne King—to Iran. In her gear was a couple hundred pounds of proto-BioStar wheat—they called it QT wheat. Her job was to get it to Warren and me."

"And what was your job?" I asked Peter.

"Warren and I had two jobs. One was to bribe the Iranian Minister of Agriculture. The other was to get the QT wheat into the hands of the farmers."

"You were meeting with the enemy in the middle of the war?" cried Patricia.

All three of us ignored Patricia. "What did the Minister of Agriculture have to do with this?" I asked.

"Well, the last thing we needed was for the Iranians to figure out that we were growing genetically modified QT wheat in country and feeding it to the locals without any kind of safety protocols. If that came out, it would have been a public relations catastrophe for the United States, and particularly for Verigro, who didn't have any authorization to be conducting these experiments in the first place."

"Then what?" I asked.

"We gave the minister five hundred thousand dollars and transferred the QT to the farmers. After that, our job was to monitor the local population for reports of widespread sickness. But nothing showed up. Not in a year, anyway. So Anne got word back to Jackie through

Errol that QT wheat was a go. The irony was that that was the message that brought down the entire house of cards."

"What do you mean?" I prompted.

"You should understand this, Charlotte. As you know, all media reports are sent through the Army censors. They had been noticing a few strange messages coming from Anne, but her last one was clearly some kind of code. So instead of passing the report on to Errol, as Anne expected, they brought her in and questioned her. She denied any involvement—and they couldn't prove she had done anything wrong—but she pointed the finger squarely at… me."

"You? Why you?" I demanded.

Peter shrugged. "That was the plan. I was the fall guy. Jackie promised me that if I went down for it and kept my mouth shut, she'd double my fee and pay me a million dollars for every year I served and give me a cushy job at Verigro when I got out. Warren's job was to go to bat for me and get my sentence reduced as much as possible. He did a pretty good job—I was only inside for six years. Believe me, a million dollars a year sounds like a lot when you're making plans. But when you're in federal prison, it's not."

I frowned. "So how did you explain where you got the money and the wheat? Surely they must have asked you that."

"They never found out about the wheat. I was indicted for improper communication with the enemy. If the Army had found out about the wheat, well… that would have been horrendous, especially for Jackie."

"So you got several million dollars." I turned to Warren. "What did you get?"

"Yes, Warren, tell us," Patricia said.

Warren finally took his hand away from his face. His voice was practically a whisper. "The Orchard," he said.

"What?" Patricia and I cried together.

"And a yearly income that keeps us in the black."

My mouth hung open. "I thought you said you inherited this place from your Uncle Horace. It was how you kept me from getting half of the place in our divorce."

"I lied," he mumbled.

"What was that?" demanded Patricia.

"I lied," Warren said, much more loudly. "All right? I lied to the both of you. This wasn't an inheritance, it was a payoff."

"Wait a minute," I said. "Peter, are you saying that Jackie Hughes used those results to push BioStar through?"

"Yes, that's exactly what I am saying," replied Peter

"And now we know that BioStar takes up to five years in the body to become toxic and cause Witko-Byrne Syndrome," I mused. "So if Jackie Hughes had done her due diligence, BioStar would never have made it to market. This really is your fault, Warren."

"What do you mean, BioStar causes WBS?" asked Patricia.

Peter told her.

"Did you know this, Warren?" asked Patricia, indignantly. "Is that why you don't grow any BioStar here? Because it causes WBS?"

"Not precisely," Warren said.

"Which means what exactly?" I pushed.

"Jackie asked me to start this place. She was the one who wanted this place to be free of transgenics. Just in case we needed a stock of natural exemplars of certain foods. It is supposed to be a safe haven for clean food."

"What about all the touchy-feely shit that goes on here?" I asked.

"Yes, Warren," Patricia said. "Is that a front for corporate greed as well?"

"No!" he said, sitting forward suddenly. "That was my idea. I wanted to make this a place of healing, not just an elaborate gene bank. And it's working. You can see it every day."

"You're a fraud!" accused Patricia. "This whole place is a fraud! My God, I was so stupid to believe that a place like this could be real. That you could be real."

"But I am real, Patricia," cried Warren, standing. "What we do here is real. It's what's going on outside that's not real. The people out there are poisoning themselves daily with genetically-engineered garbage, knowing full well that it will kill them. And they'd been doing it for thirty years before Verigro or BioStar came along. I'm providing a safe place from all that."

"If you hadn't poisoned the world, Warren," Patricia said, almost inaudibly, "then everywhere would have been safe." She turned and walked out of the office.

"Wait!" shouted Warren. "Where are you going?"

She stopped short, turned. I could see the tears streaming down her face. "Where am I going? Well, let's see. First I think I'll pack. Then I guess I'll call a town hall meeting and tell everyone here what you've been doing. Then I'm going to leave, probably with everyone else."

"No! Don't do it. Let me explain it to them. I promise I will. Please don't say anything. Let me handle it."

Patricia looked at Warren for a long time. "I used to love you, you know that?" And she turned and walked away.

Warren sat down heavily in his chair. "Get out of here," he said simply. "Both of you."

Peter stood. I escorted him back to my cottage. We had nowhere else to go.

Chapter Thirty

"What exactly are you saying?" said the man in the back row, speaking for the first time. "Is someone going to take this place away from us?"

The assembly hall was nearly full with all the adults of the Orchard in attendance. Samarie and her friends were in one of the adjacent buildings, being watched over by one of the teens. I didn't want her to know what might happen either.

I scanned the faces for any signs of danger, but I couldn't detect any. For a bunch of crazy people, they seemed remarkably calm. No one had interrupted during Warren's speech, and the questions were remarkably civil.

"I don't know, Bobby," Warren said. "The deed is in my name, but part of our income comes from Verigro. If anything happens to them…."

"Couldn't we just sell more of our harvest?" asked a woman in the middle.

"We could, Sylvia, but it would be a stretch. I haven't had a chance to crunch the numbers yet."

"Maybe you should," said a male voice from somewhere in the crowd.

"Okay, Frank, I'll do that as soon as we're done here. Look," Warren said to everyone, "I'll do anything I can to keep this place exactly the way it is. We've built a way of life here, and I don't want that to end."

"But it's a way of life built on a lie, isn't it?" called a woman from the very back. Patricia. I hadn't noticed her standing there.

The crowd grumbled in agreement. Here we go, I thought.

Warren sighed. He shuffled his feet, and I noticed some perspiration on his brow. "Look, I made some bad choices a long time ago. Choices I'm not proud of. I've already confessed them here tonight. I don't know what else I can say."

"And yet, you still seem to be missing the point," Patricia said, walking down the center aisle. "Those 'bad choices' haven't just affected us here at the Orchard. People out there are suffering, dying even, because of your 'bad choices.' How many people have you killed, Warren, with your choices? How many lives have you destroyed? How many more people will suffer for your sins?"

"Patricia," Warren said softly, "I'm sorry. I...."

"That's the best you can come up with? You're sorry?"

"I didn't know that people would be hurt," he offered.

"Oh, bullshit!" Patricia had reached the foot of the dais. She looked up at Warren with real hatred in her eyes. "You knew perfectly well that that stuff could harm people when you smuggled it into a war-torn country to experiment illegally on helpless civilians."

"It wasn't like that…" began Warren.

"God, Warren, do you really believe that?" Patricia began pacing in front of the crowd. "You accepted a huge payoff from a greedy corporation to systematically poison innocent people for an unethical experiment, which ultimately led to the deaths of what? A million people worldwide? More? Not to mention the destruction of families and the loss of countless unborn children. You're unbelievable. You don't give a shit who dies, do you?"

"Patricia…" attempted Warren.

"No! I don't want to hear it. And I'm betting that these people—your family, Warren—don't want to hear it either." She turned to the crowd. "I'm leaving this place. I'm done with the lies. Who's coming with me?"

For a moment, nothing happened. Patricia scanned the room. "You cowards!" she shouted. "Are you actually condoning what he's done?"

"We're not condoning anything," said Bobby. "But if we go out there, we'll lose everything we've built here, and you said it yourself, the disease is out there. Now, I feel for those poor souls who are suffering, but I don't want to be one of them, and if I have anything to say about it, my wife and kids won't be either. So maybe Warren needs to go. As much as we need him, I could get behind that. But given a choice between our lives here and the insanity that's going on outside, I choose the Orchard."

There were grumbles of agreement, and some conversation. Apparently, almost everyone else felt like Bobby did.

"I thought I knew you all," Patricia said. "I really did. But I don't know any of you." Patricia turned and headed for a door near the dais. She slammed it behind her.

"Thank you," Warren said. "Thank you for your support."

Everyone, and I mean everyone, including Peter and me, gaped at Warren in disbelief.

"We're not supporting you," said Bobby. "We're protecting ourselves. This is our home. Just because you got caught shouldn't mean that we should have to lose everything." Mumbles of assent. "Warren, you've been a good leader and an important part of our growth and healing. For that, we owe you. But I say it's time we had new leadership. You need to step down, Warren."

"Bobby's right," said another voice. Frank, if I remembered correctly. "You can't be in charge anymore, Warren. Why don't you just resign and save us all a lot of trouble?"

"You want me to what?" I snapped my head around to look at Warren. He had that edge in his voice, which surprised me. He didn't actually think he could fight these people, did he? "It's my land. I created this place. You can't seriously expect me to resign, can you?"

"Yes, we can," called a woman from somewhere.

Everywhere people were talking, shouting.

"I call for a vote," yelled Bobby over the noise of the crowd.

"Vote! Vote! Vote!" chanted the crowd.

"How dare you?" cried Warren. "After everything I've done for you, you're all just going to turn your backs on me? I saved you! Each and every one of you! You owe me!"

"And you owed us the truth," Frank shouted, his voice rising over the din.

By now, half the audience was standing, and they looked dangerous.

I did the only thing I could. I stepped up onto the dais and whispered in Warren's ear, "It's time to go."

Warren glared at me. He was angry, scared. For a moment, I actually felt sorry for him.

"Look at them, Warren. They're turning into a mob. Do you want to be lynched? They'll do it. Let's go." I took Warren by the elbow and nodded at Peter, who stood.

"I'm not resigning," he growled at me.

"God damn it, Warren. You can't win this one. It's time to retreat. Now let's go!" I tugged at his elbow one more time. This time, Warren let me pull him toward the door. Peter, Warren, and I walked calmly out. And to my great relief, the people let us. I turned to look at them just as we were stepping out into the night, and I could see Bobby getting up on the dais and waving his arms for order.

Chapter Thirty-One

As soon as we were outside in the cool night air, Warren turned around and punched Peter directly in the face. Peter went down, heavily, on his back. One hand held his face. The other protected his gut.

"What are you doing?" I shouted, standing over Peter protectively. I was too startled to be frightened. Warren ignored me.

"You miserable, loud-mouthed sonofabitch!" he growled at Peter. "You just couldn't keep quiet, could you? You were paid, same as the rest of us. We each held up our end of the bargain. What makes you so God-damned special that you get to break the agreement?"

"Leave him alone," I yelled, practically into Warren's nose.

Warren grabbed me by the arms and threw me to the ground. I landed on my bad arm—the pain was unbearable, and I cried out—and it collapsed under my weight. I skidded across the gravel, and I could feel the skin of my palms tearing as I attempted to right myself. Scared to death, I kept my eyes on Warren, wondering what he would do next.

"Shut up, Lotte," he cried. "Just shut up. I'm tired of you and your stories. If you had just left this alone…."

"What?" I said defiantly, my voice shaking. "So you would be able to continue living here in your little corner of paradise with everyone thinking you're a fucking hero? Did you really think you could continue living a lie forever?"

Warren swiveled his head back and forth, first looking at me, then Peter, then back to me. "It isn't a lie. What I built here is real."

"Nothing here is real, Warren. You're not a hero. You're not a healer." And then I heard myself say, "You're not even a father!"

"What?" he demanded. "What the fuck is that supposed to mean? I'm a much better father than you are a mother."

I stood, pain shooting through my arm. My hands were bleeding and raw, but I barely felt them. I clenched them into fists and stood before Warren. I wanted to be ready for another attack.

"Samarie's not your daughter, Warren."

The punch came faster than I expected it. He hit me on the left cheek, and the world spun sideways for a long, slow moment. I went down again, hard.

The world stayed sideways. I tried to get up, but this time I couldn't.

I had never been physically afraid of Warren before. He had always been my protector. But now I feared every movement he made.

I could hear Warren's feet crunch on the gravel as he came toward me. I whimpered and curled up into a ball, fearing that he was planning to kick me.

"You're a lying bitch," Warren said. I heard his feet shift, and I waited.

But instead of a kick, I heard a loud, surprised "oof" from Warren. My left eye seemed to have swollen shut, so I looked up with my right eye. Peter had his arm around Warren's neck from behind and was choking him.

Warren twisted and turned, trying to dislodge Peter, but Peter held on to Warren with surprising tenacity.

Warren brought his elbow back into Peter's stomach wound. Peter cried out and dropped to the ground. I could almost feel the blow to Peter's wound, and it made me terrified that Warren might have just killed Peter.

Warren stood over the both of us, probably trying to decide which one of us to attack next.

There was a tremendous BOOM. I flinched. Warren froze where he was.

"Stop it," a familiar voice said. Patricia's.

I could see shadows on the ground as the doors flew open and people from the meeting hall spilled out into the courtyard. I decided that it might be safe to get up. I tried to push myself up on my hands but fell back down again. Someone put their hands under my arms and lifted me to my feet.

"What the fuck is the matter with you, Warren?" Patricia shouted. She held the pump gun leveled at Warren's middle. "What were you going to do? Beat them senseless for telling us the truth about what kind of man you are? Kill them? What?"

"Patricia…" Warren began.

"Shut up!" Patricia said. "I don't want to hear it." She walked forward, still aiming the shotgun squarely at Warren. "If you have any sense, you'll go back to your house and calm down. And if you know what's good for you, you'll be gone in the morning. Do I make myself clear?"

"Patricia, this is my…."

Patricia racked the pump gun; a loud, menacing sound. One of the shells fell on the ground and clattered with a hollow, plastic clatter.

"No, it's not. This is our land now. And I'm telling you, its time you moved on. Go. Pack. Leave. You have until sunrise."

Warren evidently wasn't a complete fool. He moved his hands away from his body to show his surrender and backed away from Patricia—and, more importantly, away from the gun.

Patricia gestured with the shotgun. "Somebody get this lying bastard out of my sight," she said.

A couple of the men stepped up to Warren and whispered to him. As a group, they all turned and headed toward Warren's house.

Patricia walked toward me, dropping the barrel of the shotgun so it pointed at the ground. I heard her click the safety and watched her hand the gun to one of the nearby women.

"Are you badly hurt?" she asked me.

"I'm fine," I mumbled. I realized that my face had swollen, and I was so dizzy I could hardly stand. "Well, maybe not. Check on Peter."

"Get both of them to the infirmary," she said to the crowd.

Gentle hands guided me away from the courtyard. I was having trouble picking up my feet, but I made it all the way to the infirmary. I looked around and saw two of the men carrying Peter.

They sat me in a chair and laid Peter on the table. Patricia spent a long time examining him, poking and prodding. She was back in her element, and she seemed much calmer than she had been outside just a moment ago.

"Well, Peter," she said, "the bad news is, your nose is broken. It's not terrible. I'll be able to set it again for you. The good news is, your abdominal wound didn't open up again. As far as I can tell, you're not bleeding internally, but I can see you are tender there. That's normal. Just rest while I examine Lotte."

She turned to me and knelt next to my chair. She touched my face gently, but it hurt like hell, and I pulled back sharply.

"Take it easy," she said soothingly. "I promise I won't hurt you."

"Too late," I mumbled.

She continued to palpate my face. After the first time, it wasn't as bad. Then she checked my arm and my hands. Finally, after five minutes or so, she stood.

"The good news is," she said, "your jaw isn't broken. Nor are any of your teeth or your nose."

"What's the bad news?"

"You won't be winning any beauty contests for a few weeks." She smiled.

That was all I could take. I chuckled. Then I guffawed. Before I knew it, I was laughing so hard I could hardly breathe. I literally fell out of my chair and had to be helped up off the floor by Patricia.

"Thank you," I said when I could contain myself again. "I needed that."

"Your hands and face will heal well, as far as I can tell. Your arm is bleeding a little, but it's nothing to be worried about. I'll redress it in a moment. And I'll give you some antibiotic ointment to put on your hands. Just keep them bandaged for a day or two, and you'll be fine."

My heart finally stopped pounding so hard. "And Peter?" I asked. "He's really okay?"

"All things considered, I'd say he's in top shape. Now, unless you have a strong stomach, I suggest you go wait outside while I set Peter's nose."

"Right," I said. "I could use some fresh air anyway."

One of the men helped me as I stepped out into the night. There was a bench just outside the infirmary, and I sat down. I touched my face, which stung horribly. My arm throbbed.

I thought about what had just occurred. I don't know what would have happened if Patricia hadn't shown up with that shotgun. Would he have continued to beat us? Would he have tried to kill us? I could feel my heart start to race again. I had had enough of people trying to kill me for one lifetime. I never thought one of them would be Warren.

Some kids came running up the path—a couple of teens, and some younger children, Paige included. They were yelling, "Patricia, Patricia!"

I stood, and instantly regretted it. "Patricia's busy right now, kids. What's wrong?"

"It's Samarie," said one of the teens. "Warren just came in and grabbed her by the arm. He dragged her out. She's gone."

Chapter Thirty-Two

I was up and running before what the girl was saying really hit me. "Samarie!" I called. I ran as hard as I could to where the children were playing and burst through the doors. "Samarie!" I repeated. There were five or ten scared children, but no Samarie. "Where is she?" I demanded. But none of them knew.

I ran out into the night and shouted at the top of my lungs. "Samarie! Samarie!" My voice echoed off the walls of the valley, an eerie sound that made me think I could hear her voice. But I knew better. She was gone.

I turned around to see everyone staring at me. "He took her!" I cried. "He took her, he took her," I heard myself repeating. And then even I couldn't understand myself through the tears. I fell to the ground, the gravel rough on my knees, but I didn't care. She was gone. My God, Samarie was gone.

Patricia stepped forward, her arms open. "Come inside, Lotte."

"What the hell good will that do?" I blubbered.

"It will get you out of the cold," she replied. "Come on. We'll think of something."

I let her help me stand, and we walked back to the village. She brought me inside one of the almost identical buildings and sat me down. I was shaking and sobbing. Someone gave me something hot to drink. I couldn't tell what it was, and I didn't care.

"Wasn't someone with him?" I asked. "Didn't they see what he was doing?"

"It's not their fault, Lotte," Patricia said soothingly. "It's no one's fault but Warren's."

"We've got to find them. Find her." I pictured Warren dragging Samarie towards one of the trucks, throwing her inside, and speeding off. I continued weeping.

"He won't hurt her," Patricia said. "He loves that girl more than life."

"Maybe before," I sobbed, "but now that I told him…."

Patricia looked at me, confused. "Told him what?"

"Oh, God, I can't believe I was so stupid."

"What did you tell him, Lotte?" Patricia coaxed.

"She told him the girl wasn't his," Peter said. I looked up to see him standing over me, tissues in his nose soaking up the blood. I hadn't even heard him come in.

"She's not his daughter?" asked Patricia. She seemed just as surprised as Warren had been just before he smashed my face in.

"No," I confirmed.

"Oh, shit," Patricia said softly.

"What the fuck is that supposed to mean?" I demanded through the tears.

"Nothing," she said, collecting herself.

"Tell me!" I shouted.

Patricia shook her head. "No, he would ever do anything to her. He's the only father she's ever known. He's upset right now, but he's not the kind of person who would hurt her just to take revenge on you."

"Patricia, you don't know what kind of man he is. A week ago, I would have said exactly the same thing you did, but now we know he's not the nurturing, caring person we thought he was. Hell, what's one more dead child to him, on top of all the others?"

Patricia put her hand on my shoulder, and said, "You're upset right now, Lotte. You don't know what you are saying."

"No," I said, brushing her hand off my shoulder. "You don't know what you're saying. Look at what he did to my face, to Peter's. What do you think he would have done if you hadn't shown up with that shotgun? He would have killed us. We took everything from him. I took everything from him. Give me six good reasons why he wouldn't hurt her."

"We've got to do something," Peter said. "We've got to call the police."

"Yes," I said. "You're right. To hell with what happens to us. I've got to get Samarie back."

"Can I borrow a phone?" asked Peter.

"We don't have any phones here," Patricia said. "Warren wouldn't allow it. The only person in the whole Orchard who had a phone was Samarie."

Peter and I looked at each other at the same moment. "Samarie's phone!" we said together.

I got up and ran out of the building. Patricia was right behind me. "Where are you going?"

"My cottage! If Samarie has her phone with her, maybe we can trace it. There's a child tracker app inside." I spun around, looking at each building in turn, but I was so disoriented that I couldn't figure out which mine was.

I tipped sideways and almost went down. Patricia grabbed me by the arm and righted me. "Cody," she said to the man standing nearby, "get the Sheriff on the shortwave, and tell them what happened."

"Everything that happened?" he asked.

"Whatever it takes to get them here right away," she barked. She turned to me and said, "This way," and she and Peter helped me to my cottage.

I staggered towards my phone where it was plugged into its charger. "Someone called," I said, looking at the small screen. "Please let it be Samarie." I checked the log. It wasn't Samarie, it was George.

I activated the internet application and navigated over to the GPS tracker. "Come on, come on, come on," I chanted. It took the browser a moment to collect the data. "Shit!" I shouted. "Shit, shit!" The system couldn't find the phone. There was nothing to see.

I pulled my arm back to throw my phone across the room, but Peter caught my wrist. "I don't know what you think you're doing, Lotte," Peter said, "but you're going to need that."

"Why?" I cried. "What difference does it make anymore?"

Patricia cocked her head. "If that means you're giving up, Charlotte, it means a lot to me." She and Peter helped me to the sofa and sat me down. "You've come too far to let anyone stand in your way, let alone a pig like Warren. People are dying out there. If you give up now, how many will die tomorrow or next week or next year?"

"I can't save everyone, Patricia. I can't even save Samarie." The tears burned rivers down my face and onto my lips. "Oh, God, I want her back."

"We'll get her back," Peter said.

Someone knocked on the door to my cottage. Patricia looked to see who it was.

"Come on in, Cody," she called.

I barely heard him say, "I called the Sheriff, Patricia. They said they would be here in about twenty minutes."

"Good work, Cody," Patricia said. "See," she cooed in my ear, "everything is going to be fine."

"I seriously doubt that," I said, and I meant it.

Chapter Thirty-Three

"Are you sure this is a good idea?" asked Peter as the Sheriff's SUV rolled into the village, lights flashing.

"Peter," I said to him, "if I have to choose between our freedom and Samarie's safety, I choose Samarie." I marched out of the cottage toward the Sheriff's deputies who were stepping out of their car.

"Are you Ms. Wilson?" asked one of the deputies. His nametag read L. Duran.

"Yes," I said. I heard Peter and Patricia walk up behind me.

"What happened to your face?" asked the other deputy, who came around the front of the cruiser to stand just behind my shoulder. His nametag read G. Sanders.

"Warren happened to my face," I said. "He punched me."

"When was this?" asked Deputy Duran.

"Just before he kidnapped my daughter." I stepped back a little so I could see both deputies at once. "What I want to know is, what are you going to do to get my daughter back?"

"We're working on it," said Deputy Sanders. "I understand you're upset, Ms. Wilson, but we need you to stay calm."

I stood with my fists clenched and my leg shaking. "I am calm," I growled. "This is calm."

Patricia put her hands on my shoulders. "Why don't we go inside? It's cold out here."

"Les," Deputy Sanders said to Deputy Duran, nodding over my shoulder, "go interview the others." I turned to look. Everyone else was standing in a group not far away.

Patricia led us back into my cottage, and Peter, Patricia, and I sat on the sofa. The deputy sat in the small chair to the left.

"Before we get started, may I see your ID, Ms. Wilson?"

My heart sank. I knew he would ask for it—I even had it ready—but I knew that it would change the conversation entirely once he figured out who I was.

Dutifully, I handed over my driver's license. He scanned it with his portable, then returned it to me.

"Now, why don't you tell me what happened."

"My ex-husband, Warren Boyd, stole my little girl."

"Why do you think he took her?" asked the deputy.

Once the initial shock wore off, I realized that I couldn't lie to him. God only knows what the others were telling Deputy Duran right now. My only option was the truth. "Oh, I don't know," I said. I could hear that my voice was too loud, but I kept shouting anyway. "Maybe it was because I had just exposed him as a war criminal in front of all his friends. Maybe it was because I told him that Samarie, who he had raised as his own daughter from birth, wasn't his. Maybe it was because his fiancée was going to leave him. Maybe it was because he had just lost everything he had ever cared about."

Deputy Sanders had been typing everything I said into a small portable. Something about what I said must have finally registered, because he said, "Hold on. What did you say about Warren being a war criminal?"

Patricia put her hand on mine, silencing me, and said, "Warren conducted biological experiments on the Iranians."

Deputy Sanders looked at each one of us in turn. "Wow. Did he confess to this?"

"Yes," the three of us replied.

The deputy tapped a few more things onto his portable. "And then Warren attacked you, right?" he asked me. I nodded. He looked up at Peter and gestured toward his face. "Were you also involved in the fight with Warren?"

"Yes," Peter said. I looked at him. He still had the bloody tissues in his nose.

"I had to threaten him with a shotgun to keep him from doing something worse to them," Patricia said.

"Where was your daughter when Warren took her?"

"With some of the other children," Patricia said. "We were having a town hall meeting and we didn't want the kids involved."

Deputy Sanders opened his mouth to ask another question, but his portable beeped. He looked down at it. After reading it for a moment, he said, "Ms. Wilson, may I ask you to stand up, please?"

"Why? What's going on?"

"Ms. Wilson, you're under arrest. Please stand up." He took his handcuffs off his belt and held them loosely in his hand.

"You've got to be kidding!" shouted Patricia. "She's not the criminal here, Warren is. What possible reason could you have for arresting her?"

"There are several warrants out for her arrest, two for murder. I'm sorry," he said. He took me by the arm and hauled me to my feet. "I'm taking you into custody." He spun me around and clicked the handcuffs around my wrists.

"No," Peter said. "Look, I did it. I killed those two police officers. If you're going to arrest someone, arrest me."

Deputy Sanders looked at Peter for a long moment. He seemed to be thinking. Then he reached up and pressed the button on the microphone clipped to his shoulder. "Les, report to me, please." He pulled out another pair of handcuffs and put his hand on his gun. "You're under arrest too. We'll sort this out back at the station. Please turn around."

I couldn't help myself. I laughed. "Thank you, Peter, but that was really stupid."

"I couldn't let you go to jail for something I did," he said.

I frowned. Who was he showing off for?

The other deputy, Duran, came in, and Sanders ordered him to take custody of Peter. Together they marched us both out to the cruiser, and they stuffed us into the backseat. It was the second time in a week that I had sat in the back of a police car.

"You didn't have to do that," I said to Peter.

"Yes, I did," he insisted. "We have to stick together."

I looked at him for a long moment. "I'm sorry, Peter," I said finally.

"What for?"

I laughed. "I'm doing a really shitty job of protecting you."

"Ah, you're doing great," he said.

I continued looking at him. His face was cut, bruised, and broken. He looked like hell.

Which is why I was so surprised when I leaned over and kissed him.

Chapter Thirty-Four

"Are you looking for my daughter or not?" I demanded. I would have stood up, but the Under-Sheriff, who had decided to conduct the interview himself, chose to have my good wrist handcuffed to the chair.

"One thing at a time, Charlotte," said the Under-Sheriff, a man named Virgil White. He must have been sixty, and he looked every bit of it—out of shape, wheezing, bald, nearsighted. He constantly pushed his glasses up onto his face, just to have them slide down his nose again. "Right now we're talking about you, not your daughter."

"Well, then your priorities are fucked up, Virgil. You caught me. I'm not going anywhere. Congratulations. Now go find Samarie."

"Does that mean you're confessing?" he asked, pushing a small microphone toward me.

I paused. Where was he going with this? "Confessing to what?"

"Well, now, let's just take a look, shall we?" Virgil consulted a terminal built into the tabletop and began paging through what I gathered was an extensive report. "It seems that the charges against you include the murder of two officers of the law and kidnapping, with a whole gaggle of lesser included crimes. You could start by confessing to any of those."

"Are you telling me," I shouted, "that you won't go looking for Samarie unless I confess to that?"

"I'm not saying any such thing," wheezed Virgil. "We're giving your daughter all the attention she deserves. But let's face it, Warren Boyd is one of Gallatin County's most upstanding citizens, whereas...."

"Whereas what?" I asked. "Whereas I'm a murderer and a kidnapper? Is that it?"

"So you are confessing," he said.

"You know what, Virgil? I've had about enough of your heavy-handed manipulative bullshit. This conversation is over. I want a lawyer."

Virgil stood—a considerable task—and headed for the door. "I'm sorry you feel that way, Charlotte. I think you might like to know that, seeing as it's nighttime on a weekend, you may be in our lockup for a couple of days before we can track down a lawyer for you. Sweet dreams."

He stepped through the doorway and began to close the door. "What was that?" he called to some unseen person. "No, the prisoner ain't accepting no phone calls.

What do you think this is, the Ritz? Tell 'em to call back during business hours." There was a pause. "Oh. Why didn't you say so? Bring it in here."

Virgil came back into the room, followed by a clerk carrying a small, cordless speakerphone. The clerk departed, leaving me, Virgil, and the speakerphone in the room.

"It seems you have a friend in high places, Charlotte." He reached over and pressed a button on the speakerphone. "This is Under-Sheriff Virgil White" he said. "I got Ms. Charlotte Wilson here with me. Go ahead."

"Under-Sheriff?" said a familiar voice. Jackie's. "I'm wondering if you would give Ms. Wilson and me some privacy." I could feel the hairs on my arms stand up.

"Well, I don't know about that," hedged Virgil.

"Please, Under-Sheriff. I'd consider it a personal favor." She said it sweetly, but with authority.

"Uh," he said uncertainly. "I suppose I could give you a couple of minutes." He went for the door again. "I'll be back in five," he said in what I'm sure he thought was a menacing voice.

"Thanks again, Under-Sheriff. I don't forget favors."

Virgil closed the door behind him.

"Charlotte?" Jackie began.

"What do you want?" I demanded.

I could almost hear her smirk. "I understand you've been having some personal difficulties. First and foremost, I want to offer my deepest sympathies. Not having children myself, I can't even begin to imagine what it must be like to have one kidnapped."

My blood froze. "How did you know about that?"

"Oh, one hears things. Kidnappings are big news, even kidnappings in Montana. But as a reporter, you know that better than I do, don't you?"

"If you had anything to do with Samarie…" I attempted.

"Please, Ms. Wilson, I didn't call you to upset you. I thought perhaps we might be able to find some common ground."

"Common ground? You have got to be kidding me, Jackie. What the fuck do you want from me, anyway?"

"I see you would like to dispense with the pleasantries and get right down to business. So be it. I know you think you may have a story to tell regarding Verigro."

"Ha!" I interrupted. "You bet your ass I do. Peter told me everything."

"You might want to seriously reconsider pursuing that story based on his word alone. It may not lead you where you think will."

"What's that supposed to mean?"

"What I mean is that Verigro is a very well-respected corporation. We have connections all over the world. Many millions of lives depend on our products."

"And how many lives have been destroyed by your products? Do you even know the number?"

Jackie paused. "I think you are mistaken. Our products save lives. Verigro feeds the globe."

"Don't give me your slogans, Jackie. I know all about you and your global reach. Peter told me all about your little experiments in Iran, and Warren confirmed it."

"Is that the same Warren who has kidnapped your daughter and disappeared?"

"You think that's going to stop me?" I demanded. "I'll get the proof I need, and when I do, you will be sorry you ever heard of me. I'll bring down your paper castle. You're going to pay for all the lives you've ruined, the people you've killed. Do you read me?"

Jackie paused again, longer this time. "I think perhaps we aren't communicating. I didn't call you to threaten you, Charlotte. I called to offer you a deal."

It was my turn to pause. Did she actually think she could bribe me? I couldn't believe she would even think that I would take a deal from her. Suddenly I wished Nick were here. He'd have come up with the perfect way to tell her to go screw herself.

"Charlotte?" said Jackie. "Are you still there?"

"I'm not interested in your deal, Jackie. You're going down. I swear to God, I will see you burn for your crimes."

As I stabbed the disconnect button, I could hear Jackie cry "Wait." But it was too late for her. I was determined to follow through on my promise to bring this story to the public. Not even Jackie could stop me.

Chapter Thirty-Five

"Wake up!"

I opened my eyes. I didn't remember falling asleep. I had been pacing most of the night. Light was streaming in the small, high windows of the jail. I stretched and flipped the blanket off me and put my feet on the cold concrete floor.

"What's going on?" I asked.

"You have a visitor," said the deputy who stood at the door of my cell.

"Is it my lawyer?"

"No. Lawyers don't usually come on Sundays. Get dressed," she said, opening the door, "I'll take you to her."

"Her? Who is it? Is it Samarie? Did you find my daughter?" I threw on my clothes and jammed my feet into my shoes.

"Sorry, hon, but we haven't found your daughter yet. Sign in sheet says her name is Leeds. P. Leeds."

"I don't know anyone named Leeds," I said, following the deputy closely.

The deputy shrugged. "That's what it says."

She led me into the visitation room. Patricia was waiting there, behind a pane of very thick glass.

I picked up the phone on my side of the glass. "Patricia," I said. "What are you doing here?"

"I couldn't just sit at the Orchard and do nothing. After the deputies took you away, we held another town hall meeting. Remember Bobby? Well, he's the treasurer. He broke open the coffers. I'm here to bail you and Peter out."

"I..." I began, but I couldn't find the words.

"You don't have to say anything, Charlotte. It was the least we could do, especially after what Warren did."

"That's not your fault," I started again.

"Yes, it is. If I hadn't flipped out on Warren when I found out what he did in Iran, maybe..."

"Patricia," I interrupted, "it's not your fault. Make no mistake, this is all Warren's fault. If he hadn't lied to us all this time, things would have been very different."

"I can't believe how stupid I was to buy his bullshit about the healing powers of the Earth. Him and his stupid diet! Do you know how long it's been since I've had a decent cheeseburger? I thought he knew what he was talking about, but it was all part of the lie, wasn't it?" Tears welled up in her eyes. I could tell she was barely holding it together.

"Don't be so quick to judge," I said. "How long have you been at the Orchard?"

"Next month, it's three years," she replied.

"I'll tell you something, Patricia. I've been watching Warren build the Orchard since he started it seven years ago. As crazy as all his theories about how to eat and live may have seemed, I'm convinced he was really on to something."

"You don't have any reason to defend him," she said.

"I'm not. Let me ask you something: how many colds and flus have you had to treat while you were the doctor at the Orchard?"

"I don't know. Not too many, I guess."

"I'm guessing none. And there are what? Two hundred people living there?"

"Two hundred and fifty-seven," she sniffed.

"Two hundred and fifty-seven," I repeated. "And how many deaths were there in those three years?"

"Fred Johnson drowned in the lake a year ago," she offered.

"But no one died of a disease, did they?"

Patricia paused to think. "No, they didn't. You think it was Warren's diet?"

"Yes, I do. Samarie used to get colds all the time while she was living with me in Seattle. She never once had one during her summers at the Orchard. Ever since she was a baby, she's been a fanatic about organic everything, same as Warren. I can't get her to eat anything with wheat, and nothing that isn't certified organic. I thought she had celiac disease until she told me it was because of Warren and his Orchard diet. You know what I think was going on? Warren was keeping her from eating BioStar, her and all of you. And you know what? Samarie hasn't had a cold—well, more than a sniffle—since then. I started eating that way just to keep Samarie from harassing me. I lost weight—a lot of weight. I'm in almost as good of shape as I was when I was embedded in Warren's unit in Iran. And look at you! You're gorgeous."

Patricia actually blushed. "It wasn't bullshit?"

"You're the doctor," I said. "You tell me."

She thought for a long time. "So, other than being with Warren, I really didn't waste three years of my life, did I?"

"No, you didn't," I said reassuringly. "Warren may have been a lying sack of shit, but he wasn't stupid. He got some things right."

"Like Samarie," Patricia said. "He really was a good father to her."

"I know," I said. There wasn't anything else to say.

"Do you mind if I ask who Samarie's real father is?"

I hesitated. "You don't know him."

"All right," she said, and she dropped it.

I stared down at my hands. "Do you think Samarie's all right?"

"Warren won't hurt her," Patricia said with absolute certainty. "He's just upset. When he comes to his senses, he'll bring her back."

"He better," I scowled. "If that sonofabitch so much as puts a bruise on her, he'll have a hell of a lot more to worry about than genocide and kidnapping charges!"

"I still can't believe that he would do that. Why would he get involved in something as evil as all this?"

"Well, Jackie Hughes is rich. He probably couldn't resist the money. Without her, Warren wouldn't have had anything but an Army pension. Now he won't even have that." Then something occurred to me. "You know, if he's so dependent on Jackie Hughes…."

"Then that's probably where he's headed!" completed Patricia.

"Holy shit." I stood up, went to the door, and pounded on it. "Deputy! Deputy!"

The door opened a moment later. The deputy had her club in hand. "Quiet down. What's the matter?"

"I need to see the Under-Sheriff. I know where my ex-husband is headed."

"Where?" asked the deputy.

"Milwaukee," I said.

Chapter Thirty-Six

"He's probably already there," I said.

Virgil drummed his fingers on the table of the interrogation room. "Charlotte, I told you before, we've got the whole damned country looking for your daughter. There can't be that many twenty-year-old white Ford F-150 biodiesel pickups on the road right now, and when your ex-husband gets caught—and he will—I'm sure your daughter will be safe and sound."

Patricia put her hands down flat on the table and stood. "Yes, but now you know where to look."

Virgil hefted himself out of the chair and shuffled over to the door. "Ladies, I appreciate the information, but I would also be obliged to you if you wouldn't try to do our jobs for us." He opened the door and said into the hallway, "Emily, would you escort Ms. Wilson here back to her cell."

"Under-Sheriff," said a female voice from outside—Emily, I guessed—"the FBI is on the phone."

Virgil huffed. "It's about damned time. I'll take it in my office."

"It's not for you," said Emily, "it's for Ms. Wilson."

Virgil turned and glared at me. He hesitated at the door, then came back inside. "Bring it in here," he said. He lumbered back to his seat.

"Do you mind, Virgil?" I said. "It's private."

"It ain't your lawyer, so it ain't private."

I started to argue, but Patricia put her hand on mine. I took the hint. Emily brought the cordless speakerphone into the interrogation room and set it down on the table.

"This is Under-Sheriff Virgil White. To whom do I have the pleasure of speaking?"

"Under-Sheriff, this is Agent George Martinez, FBI. I was expecting Charlotte Wilson. I need to speak to her right away."

"Go ahead," said Virgil. "She's right here."

"Charlie? You there?"

"I'm here George," I replied. "And I've got Patricia Leeds and the Under-Sheriff here with me. Is that okay?"

"I guess it's going to have to be. I got your message, but it doesn't make any sense. Warren kidnapped Samarie?"

"Yes, last night," I said.

"Why in the world would he do that?"

"It's a long story," I sighed.

"Make it short," George said.

Patricia squeezed my hand again. "Agent Martinez, this is Patricia Leeds. I'm Warren's ex-fiancée. It turns out that Warren is a war criminal, and now everyone knows it. When I found out, I broke off the engagement and was going to leave the Orchard. Then Lotte told Warren that he wasn't Samarie's father. Is that sufficient motive?"

"Whoa!" George said. "Maybe that was too short. Start again from the top. What's this about Warren being a war criminal?"

"George," I said, "this isn't a really good time to talk."

Virgil looked up at me sharply. "I think it's the perfect time to talk."

"George," I said again, "I need you to come get Peter and me. How soon can you be here? I'll explain everything when I see you."

"I'm already on my way. I should be landing in Bozeman in about thirty minutes."

"Hold on a second, Agent Martinez. Ms. Wilson here and Peter Youngs are in my custody, and that's the way I plan to keep it until I get to the bottom of this. There ain't no reason for you to come here."

"Under-Sheriff, I don't want to fight with you. I want to thank you for your excellent work and dedication," George said in a friendly voice. "We'll handle the transfer of custody of your prisoners when I arrive. Do you have any questions?"

"No, no questions. You're pulling rank. You think I'm some kind of hick who doesn't know his job. Well, I do know my job. You're going to need an okay from the Gallatin County Sheriff before I release my prisoners to you."

"You're absolutely right, Under-Sheriff. That's why a copy of the release should be on your desk right about now."

Virgil stared at the phone, apparently at a loss for words. Then he grumbled. "Fine. As soon as I verify the Sheriff's authorization, I'll prepare the prisoners for travel. Is that fast enough for you?"

"Thank you, Under-Sheriff. Charlie, are you going to be okay until I get there?"

"I'll be fine," I said.

"All right. See you soon." The speakerphone clicked, and the little light went out.

Virgil stabbed a button on the speakerphone and growled, "Emily, go get Prisoner Youngs ready for travel. And collect Prisoner Wilson's belongings and bring them and Youngs' in here."

"Yes, Under-Sheriff," said the disembodied voice. The little light went out again.

I turned to Patricia. "I need a favor. Can you go to the Orchard and bring back Peter's and my things?"

She smiled. "I have them in the car. Is that fast enough for you?"

I leaned over and hugged her, which probably surprised her as much as it did me. "Thank you," I said.

"All right, all right," said Virgil. "Now that your little love-fest is over, you got some paperwork needs filling out before you get released."

"Thank you, Virgil," I said.

Chapter Thirty-Seven

The engines of the FBI's corporate jet were barely audible as a slight whistling whine. The overstuffed chair I sat in swiveled and I turned it to stare out the window, thinking of Samarie. She would have loved riding in this plane.

"So far, no reports of Warren or Samarie," George said, scanning his portable. "I've got the Milwaukee office alerted, and they are already searching for them. We've got agents outside Verigro's offices and Hughes's home. If Warren shows up at either one, we'll get him."

"What about Jackie Hughes?" asked Peter.

"What about her?" replied George.

"Jackie is responsible for all of this. Aren't you going to arrest her?"

George ran his fingers through his thick, dark hair. His tie was already loosened, and he had taken off his coat almost as soon as the jet had taken off from Bozeman airport.

"It's not that simple," he said. "We only have your word that Hughes has done anything wrong. Whether I believe your story or not, we don't have enough proof to convince a judge—federal or otherwise—to sign a warrant for her arrest. Everything you've told me…. Look, I know you two believe it, but I just can't move forward on your word—which frankly adds up to nothing more than a bunch of wild accusations."

Peter stood up and began pacing the center aisle. "What more proof do you need?"

"How about some documentation? You've been telling me that you have terabytes of reports that back up your allegations, but so far you haven't shown me a shred of evidence."

"It's all in Verigro's database. But I can get to it. All I need is a terminal with access to the internet."

"We've got internet access right here," George said. "If you really have those reports, then now would be a good time to get them."

Peter reached into his pocket and pulled out the decapitated figurine of Marvin the Martian. "May I?" he asked.

George placed the portable in front of Peter and said, "Be my guest."

Peter picked it up and inserted Marvin into one of the data ports. He swiped the track pad, and a keyboard appeared. He quickly typed something and waited. George and I looked over his shoulder.

Verigro's corporate logo appeared on the screen, along with a request for a username and password. Peter tapped in his credentials, making a quick staccato beat. The screen changed, showing a search function.

"There, I'm in," Peter said.

"All right," replied George. "Let's see the proof."

Peter typed the term "applecorpse" into the search function, and triumphantly clicked enter.

"Applecorpse?" I asked.

"Trust me," Peter said. "You'll see."

We waited a long moment, and finally the search returned a result. "Search term not found," it said.

"What the hell?" Peter typed another term in— "breezeway" this time—and pounded the enter key.

"Search term not found."

"Why don't you just try BioStar?" asked George.

"Because nothing useful will come up—only the publicly available reports, which are all fabrications."

George stood up and began walking around the cabin. "So where's your proof, Peter?"

"It's supposed to be here. Let me try something else." He tapped a command into the portable and waited. I watched as the screen changed to a colorful spreadsheet with numbers and letters in each cell. It showed mostly green cells, with the occasional yellow and red. A few of the cells were white.

"What's this?" asked George.

"It's the drive matrix in the server. Kind of a map of all the storage drives connected to Verigro's system." Peter ran his finger over the screen of the portable. "I hid the reports on a dozen of these drives, redundantly, so that it couldn't be wiped out all at once."

"So? Where is it?" demanded George.

Peter ignored him and scanned the spreadsheet. Every time there was a white cell, his finger would stop and he would curse. "Fuck!" he said finally.

"What's wrong?" I asked softly.

"Those bastards didn't just erase the data, they physically pulled the drives." He looked at me, then at George. "If it was there, I might be able to retrieve it. But this way it's gone. I can't get to it."

I leaned back in my chair and covered my eyes with my hand. "Where does that leave us?"

"It leaves you two facing multiple murder charges, and Warren facing federal kidnapping charges. As far as Jackie Hughes is concerned, even if she did what you said she did, we can't prove it, so she's going to get away with it."

"Yeah, her and Haley Bowen and Errol Foster," I said as I stared out the window.

"Hey, what about Errol?" asked Peter.

"What about him?" I asked.

Peter turned to George and said, "If Errol Foster were to come forward and back up my story, would that give you enough to get a warrant for Jackie and a subpoena for those records?"

"Why would Errol come forward?" I asked.

"Because I'm betting he never signed on to be responsible for Witko-Byrne Syndrome. I certainly didn't.

Isn't that why he gave you the go-ahead to get the story about BioStar?"

I looked up at him. "I suppose."

"Besides, don't you have some special influence with him? You're sleeping with him, after all."

"God damn it, Peter," I shouted, "I am not sleeping with Errol Foster. Nick was exaggerating when he said I had some special influence over Errol. It just isn't true." I took a deep breath and said, "Besides, if Errol was wrapped around my finger, why would he tell Jackie Hughes where to send her goons to come kill us back in Milwaukee? Answer me that."

Peter remained silent. George went back to his seat and stared at me.

"What?" I demanded.

"Let's look at this another way," George said, "there were six people involved with this conspiracy in Iran, right? You," he said, indicating Peter, "Jackie Hughes, Errol Foster, Haley Bowen, Anne King, and Warren Boyd. If we can get just one of the others to back up this story of yours, we'd have something."

Peter turned to me and said, "Didn't you record the meeting on your phone?"

"Oh, my God. I've got it right here." I dug into my bag and pulled out my phone. I opened a small cover and popped out the memory card and handed it over to George. He inserted the card into a reader on the side of the portable and brought up the recordings I made of Peter's and Warren's confessions.

We listened for a long time. George's face was like a statue through it all. Near the end, though, he began shaking his head. By the end of the recording, he had placed his head in his hands. "No, this is no good," he said.

"What do you mean, it's no good?" I demanded. "Everything you need is right there," I said, pointing at the portable.

"And I'm telling you it won't help at all. After that scandal with President Ellsworth, they raised the bar on the burden of proof when accusing public figures of wrongdoing."

"So what?" I replied. "That should be enough to meet the burden of proof."

"I'm telling you, Charlie, it doesn't. Peter and Warren admit they conducted biological experiments and bribed Iranian officials during the war, and that would be enough to arrest them. But Haley Bowen was Secretary of Agriculture for almost 16 years, and Jackie Hughes is running for Senate, so they're covered by the Public Figures Act. I'll bet you a dollar that Errol Foster could successfully argue that he qualifies, too. That leaves Anne King, and what good would it do us to arrest her? She isn't involved in these kidnappings and murders, is she?"

"Are you telling me that Jackie and Errol are above the law?" demanded Peter.

"No, not above the law. But we need concrete evidence against them to start an investigation, let alone get a warrant or make an arrest. In a case of your word against theirs, the Public Figures Act sides with them."

"Meaning, we're screwed," I said.

"Maybe not," Peter said.

"What?" asked George.

"I have some other evidence, physical evidence, of BioStar's toxicity. Would that be enough to get an investigation started?"

"It might," mused George. "Where is it?"

"Back at my house," he said.

"All right. When we touch down in Milwaukee, we'll head over to the FBI office to get our bearings. Then we'll go to your house and collect the evidence. Good enough?"

Peter relaxed. "Works for me."

"All right," I said. "What about Samarie?"

"I promise we'll let you know as soon as anyone hears anything. We can't make things go any faster than that."

I gritted my teeth. I couldn't think of anything to say that would be the slightest bit helpful. I wanted to get Samarie back, and all this other stuff was just a distraction. I went for something socially innocuous.

"Thank you, George," I said.

"Yes, thank you," Peter agreed.

Chapter Thirty-Eight

Minnesota looked pretty much like the Dakotas from thirty thousand feet. Apart from the lakes, it was browns and greens, with small populated areas dotted around.

George sat at the front of the cabin, talking quietly to his boss. Peter and I sat near the back, and I looked out the window.

I refused to look at him. "May I ask you something?"

"Anything you like."

"Why all the theatrics with having Nick and me protect you? Why not just go to the FBI?"

Peter looked out of the side window and was quiet for a while. "Well, I knew that Jackie had the police in her back pocket. Who knew how far her reach went? She's friends with a lot of powerful people—presidents, cabinet members, congressmen—so it wasn't much of a stretch to believe that she had connections in the FBI."

"But I thought you knew her whole operation," I said.

"Don't kid yourself, Charlotte. Jackie never told me a damned thing. Everything I knew about the operation at Verigro I had to figure out on my own."

I looked around the cabin. "You know something, Peter. I was never claustrophobic before, but despite the windows, this cabin is getting to me. After all the interrogation rooms I've been in over the last week, I've gotten sick of sitting in little blank rooms, waiting for someone else to get around to paying attention to me. I think I'm going to start bouncing off the walls if I have to put up with this much longer."

"You get used to it," Peter said.

I turned to him. "It must have been tough in prison," I said sympathetically.

"It wasn't all that bad, I suppose. And when I was released from prison, there was a plane ticket to Milwaukee waiting for me. When I arrived, a limo picked me up and took me to Jackie's offices. She had a new identity waiting for me, a job, a bank account full of money, and that big house in Whitefish Bay. She took care of everything. One day I'm Peter McCormick, federal convict, and the next I'm Peter Youngs, executive with one of the most successful biotech companies in the country."

"But... Jackie was the one who sent you to prison. How could you trust her?"

"No, you have it backwards," Peter said. "The United States Government sent me to prison. Jackie kept her word and took care of me. We were even."

"If everything was so good between you and Jackie," I said, "then why did you turn on her?"

"Because I never signed on to poison people. In the Army, I understood that the job may include killing the enemy, but the people who are suffering and dying from Witko-Byrne aren't the enemy. When I found out that BioStar and WBS were cause and effect, I couldn't stay quiet. I had to do something."

"And you called me?" I asked.

Peter frowned. "Sure. Why not?"

"Why not?" I repeated, surprised. "Oh, I don't know. Maybe because I am the ex-wife of one of your co-conspirators, and the employee of another one. I can't think of anyone less suited to be trusted than me."

"You don't understand," Peter said, smiling. "That's what made you so perfect. Errol and Warren would have never believed me if I had gone to them with my concerns about BioStar. They would have thought I was just trying to get more out of my deal than I deserved. But if you brought the story to them, they had to believe you, right? I mean, what could you possibly gain from bringing this story to light?"

"Evidently nothing," I grumbled. "At first, I thought Nick and I would be looking at a Pulitzer, and we both know what happened to him. Now, if I'm lucky, when this is all over, I'll get my daughter back, I'll still have a job, and I won't go to prison for the deaths of those two policemen. You're right, what could I possibly have to gain from this?" I sat heavily in one of the institutional chairs and rested my head in my hand.

"I'm really sorry about all the trouble I've caused you, Charlotte," Peter said.

I looked at him for what seemed a long time. "Don't be," I said finally. I took his hand. "You're doing the right thing. The big picture is, it doesn't really matter what happens to me and you. A hundred million people have a disease that, at its mildest, will ruin their lives, and at the worst, will kill them. A million new cases are reported every year. At that rate, the human race would be facing its own extinction within ten or twenty years. But now that you have come forward all those lives will be saved. You're going to be a hero."

Peter sighed. "I don't want to be a hero."

"What do you want then?" I asked.

"This," he said, and he leaned in to kiss me.

George stood up right then and came aft. Peter immediately pulled back and tried to look innocent.

"Charlie," he said, taking the seat in front of mine and swiveling it to face me. "I've got some news for you."

"Is it about Samarie?" I asked excitedly.

"Sort of," he hedged.

"Sort of?" I repeated. "What does 'sort of' mean? What happened?"

"We've found Warren," George said.

"Oh, my God. Is Samarie all right?"

"We don't know."

"What the fuck do you mean, you don't know?" I shouted.

"There's no easy way to say this, Charlie. Warren is dead, and Samarie isn't with him."

Chapter Thirty-Nine

The helicopter was waiting for us as soon as we touched down at Mitchell Field. The short flight south took us over a small town where I could see police lights covering a small section of the ground, next to a large warehouse. The one in Bannockburn. The one where Nick died. I pressed the microphone of my headset to my mouth and said, "What are we doing here?" The engine and rotor sound from the helicopter deafened me, even through the thick headphones.

"This is where they found Warren," he said simply.

George and I made eye contact. Nick and those two police detectives had died here, and then Warren. There was no way that was a coincidence.

"What the hell was he doing here?" I asked as we came in for a landing.

"We don't know yet, Charlie. We don't know much of anything. Look, I need you to stay in the helicopter while I go find out. I promise to tell you anything we discover as soon as we have it." The helicopter touched down, and George jumped out.

I opened the door and shouted at him. "I'm coming with you."

"I don't think that's a very good idea. You don't want to see this."

"I've been to crime scenes before. I promise I will stay out of the way. I can't just sit in the helicopter and wait while my little girl is out there somewhere."

"If it helps," yelled Peter, "I'll keep her out of the way. I think you should let her go."

George grumbled, "No, I want you to stay in the helicopter. Peter, do me a favor and keep her here." George closed the door behind him.

I could see Warren's truck surrounded by about seven policemen and crime scene specialists. Both doors were open, but I couldn't see anything beyond that. A crowd had gathered at the periphery of the crime scene tape. I spotted a few reporters in the midst of the crowd. At least one of them was a Foster Media Network reporter.

I glanced at Peter. He was looking around at the crime scene, but more importantly, not at me. I didn't hesitate. I threw off my headphones and jumped out of the already opened door.

"Charlotte!" I heard Peter say as I dashed away.

I walked quickly toward the FMN truck. As soon as I got there, I poked my head inside. "Hey," I said.

"Can I help you?" said the producer, a tiny woman wearing a baseball cap that was twice as big as her head.

"I'm Charlotte Wilson, FMN Seattle."

"What are you doing here?" she asked. "And what happened to your face?"

"The deceased is named Warren Boyd. He's my ex-husband. The last I saw him, he was in the process of kidnapping my daughter." I let the producer fill in the blanks.

She stabbed a button on her console and said, "Kevin, Lowell, get back to the truck. Now!" She stepped down from the truck. "I'm Alana Goldman, the producer. I'm so sorry for your loss," she said.

"Charlotte, what are you doing?" asked Peter, finally catching up with me. "George said to wait in the helicopter!"

"He means FBI Agent George Martinez," I informed Alana. She dutifully wrote that down.

The reporter and his cameraman arrived back at the truck a moment later. "What's up, Alana?" asked the reporter.

"Kevin," said Alana, "this is the deceased's ex-wife, Charlotte Wilson. She's an FMN reporter from Seattle."

The cameraman instantly brought his camera up to cover me and Peter. I saw the little red light come on.

"Hey! I know you," Kevin said. "You did that report on political corruption in Muncie a few months back."

"Thank you," I said. "I'm ready to give an interview anytime you are."

"You're going to do what?" Peter demanded. We all ignored him.

Kevin straightened his coat. "Come over here," he said. He maneuvered me to a spot where the camera had a clear shot of the crime scene in the background. Alana came up to Kevin and had a few words with him. I presumed she was filling him in on what she had learned. Kevin nodded.

"Charlotte," Peter said, "this is a very bad idea. George isn't going to like this at all."

"I know what I am doing," I told him as I tried to straighten my hair as best I could.

Kevin nodded to the cameraman, Lowell. "Rolling," said Lowell.

"This is Kevin Reno, reporting from Bannockburn, Illinois. I'm here at the scene of what appears to be the suicide of a man named Warren Boyd, who is suspected of kidnapping his own daughter. I have with me veteran reporter Charlotte Wilson, who is the deceased's ex-wife. Charlotte, what can you tell us about what's happening here?"

"Thank you, Kevin. First of all, I want to put out an appeal to anyone who might know the whereabouts of my daughter. Her name is Samantha Marie Boyd, though she answers to the name Samarie. She's eleven years old, has long, brown hair and hazel eyes. She weighs about ninety pounds. And she's probably scared out of her mind right now."

"Do you have a picture of her?" asked Kevin.

"I might. Peter, could you check my bag?" I asked.

"When did Mr. Boyd kidnap her?" prompted Kevin.

"About forty hours ago. He took her from Bozeman, Montana, and we guessed that he was headed for Milwaukee."

"Why did he kidnap her?"

"I presume he kidnapped her because he was distraught. Warren is the owner and leader of a commune called The Orchard. They help people with post-traumatic stress disorder recover through work with the land. Warren's followers just found out that Warren had allegedly committed some crimes in the past, and they had voted him out as leader. His fiancée was leaving him, and I had told him that Samarie was another man's daughter. That's a lot to handle in the space of an hour."

"Why do you think he was headed to Milwaukee?" asked Kevin.

I hesitated. If I said it, there was no taking it back.

"Because Jackie Hughes is there."

"Jackie Hughes? The Senatorial candidate? How is she connected with this?"

"She was allegedly the leader of the conspiracy that led Warren to commit his crimes." I said it quickly, with confidence.

"That's a pretty strong allegation to make the day before the election. What proof do you have of this?"

I turned to Peter. "This is Peter Youngs, Chief Operating Officer at Verigro, Jackie Hughes's company. He can explain everything to you."

"Charlotte," whispered Peter, "what are you doing?"

I said, "You wanted me to get this story out, Peter. Here's your big chance."

"Yeah, about BioStar."

Kevin and Lowell immediately turned their attention to Peter.

"Is this true?" asked Kevin. "Is Jackie Hughes involved in a criminal conspiracy?"

"I, uh," Peter said.

I put my hand on Peter's arm. "It's okay, Peter. Just tell them what you told me."

Peter looked like a deer in headlights. Finally, he found his voice. "Yes, it's true."

I saw someone running toward us, who turned out to be George. "Whoa!" he said. Lowell turned the camera on George. "This interview is over," George shouted. "Whatever they are saying is part of an ongoing investigation. Turn that camera off."

"Who are you?" asked Kevin. I noticed that Lowell was still recording.

"This is Agent George Martinez of the FBI," I said.

"That's right, and I'm telling you to turn off that camera!"

"Agent Martinez," said Kevin, "we have a First Amendment right to be here. You can't order us to end the interview."

"Maybe not, but I can take my prisoners back into custody," he said.

"Prisoners?" asked Kevin, incredulously. "What have they been charged with?"

"That's none of your business." George turned to Peter and me. "Are you going to come back to the helicopter, or do I have to put the handcuffs on you again?"

"I really don't think that's going to help," I said to George.

"Damn it, Charlie," he said, pulling out his handcuffs. "Why can't you just do what you're told?" He snapped one bracelet over my good wrist, and the other over Peter's. "We're going back to the helicopter," he said, and he shoved us in that direction.

Peter still held my bag. I could hear my phone ringing inside of it.

"Give me that," I said, and Peter did. I pulled the phone out—it was a bit awkward with one hand chained to Peter's—and looked at it. "Oh, my God."

"Who is it?" asked Peter.

"It's Samarie!" I shouted.

Chapter Forty

"Mommy?" whispered Samarie.

"Samarie? Where are you, baby?"

"I don't know," she said. I could hear that she had been crying. It took everything I had to not do the same. "Somebody took me. I think they hurt Daddy. Is Daddy okay?"

"He's fine, Pumpkin. Are you hurt?"

"No," she said. "I'm okay, I guess. I'm scared."

"I know, Samarie, I know. I'm coming to find you right now." I looked at George and mouthed "GPS" at him. He ran to the helicopter and retrieved a portable. "Listen," I said into the phone, "I need you to do something for me. It's very important. No matter what happens, I need you to leave your phone on. Can you do that?"

"Okay," she said. "When are you going to be here? I don't like this place."

George held the portable up for me, and I held the phone between my shoulder and my ear. I typed in my credentials for the GPS tracker app on Samarie's phone.

"Ask her to describe where she is," George said.

"Samarie, can you tell me what it looks like where you are? Can you describe it?"

"I guess so. It's a big, bright room. There's a table in the middle, and some chairs. And I can see Lake Michigan."

I entered my credentials and waited. After what seemed like forever, the GPS tracker came up.

"She's in Chicago," George said, taking the portable away from me.

"Errol," Peter and I said together.

I took the phone from my shoulder and said, "Okay, Samarie. We know where you are now."

"When will you be here?"

"Just a little while, baby, I promise."

George looked at me and said, "All right. We have her. You need to hang up now."

"No!" I cried. "I'm not letting her go."

"It's too dangerous. If she gets caught with the phone, who knows what they'll do to her. Tell her to hang up but leave the phone on. Do it, Charlie."

"Samarie?" I said into the phone.

"Mommy, I don't want to be here. Please come get me. These people scare me."

"I know, Pumpkin, I know. But I need you to be brave for me. Can you do that?"

"Yes," she said, but I could hear her voice crack again.

"All right. I need you to hang up now. If the people who have you find the phone, they'll turn it off and…"

"What the hell are you doing?" said a voice on Samarie's end of the line. The phone suddenly went dead.

"Oh, my God!" I screamed.

"What happened?" asked Peter and George together.

"Someone found her! They hung up the phone. Oh, God. Please don't let them hurt her!"

George looked back at the portable. "Fuck," he said. "The signal is gone."

"Do you know where she is?" I asked frantically.

"I think so." He pulled out his phone and began dialing. "I'm calling the Chicago office. They can be there in ten minutes."

"Is that fast enough?" asked Peter.

"I don't know," George said. The Chicago office must have picked up, because he turned away from us and began speaking rapidly.

"Tell me she's going to be all right," I said to Peter.

Peter put his arms around me and said, "They're doing everything they can. They'll find her."

I held on to him tight and cried.

I heard Peter say to someone, "Did you get all that?" He sounded angry.

I turned to see Kevin, Lowell, and Alana standing behind me. Lowell was recording everything, and Kevin had his microphone extended to get every word. They looked at each other and Kevin pulled back the microphone.

I released my hold on Peter and pulled back a bit. "Go easy on them, Peter. As a reporter, I would have done the same thing."

George looked at me expectantly. "Charlie? Are you coming or not?"

I didn't need to be asked twice. Peter and I ran as fast as we could back to the helicopter. As I ran, I prayed that the kidnappers wouldn't hurt Samarie.

Chapter Forty-One

George was talking to the Chicago office during the entire helicopter flight to the city, about twenty minutes in total. I could hardly sit still. Peter allowed me to grip his hand the whole time. I hoped I wasn't hurting him too much, but at that particular moment, I didn't really care.

The helicopter set down on the roof of a tall building somewhere near the middle of Downtown Chicago. I could see the Sears Tower from where we were, and I could see Lake Michigan. For all I knew, we had just landed on the building where she was being held.

We were met by a man and a woman in dark suits with headsets in their ears. I presumed they were FBI. Once we were off the roof and in the elevator, George said, "Charlie, I'm sending you and Peter with Agent Patel here back to the FBI office. You'll be safe with her."

"No, I'm coming with you," I insisted.

"Charlie," George said, as calmly as he could, "I can't let you do that. Samarie is in too much danger. We don't know what these people are going to do to her. You need to leave this to the professionals. Believe me, if anyone can get her back, the FBI can."

"But what if you need me to… I don't know, negotiate or something?" I was grasping at straws, I knew, but I had to do something.

George smiled in what I guessed he thought was a reassuring way. "That's why God invented telephones."

"I can't just sit around doing nothing, George. Please!"

"I'm sorry, Charlie. I've got orders from my boss not to let you anywhere near this situation. Go with Patel. Everything will be all right."

Before I could say anything else, the elevator doors opened into the garage. Two black SUVs were waiting there—one for George and the male agent, and one for Peter, me, and Agent Patel.

Just as George was about to jump into his SUV, he turned to Patel and said, "If the kid calls Charlie back, let me know immediately."

"Roger that, Martinez." Then she looked at us and said, "Let's go."

"Do you think you could do something about these handcuffs?" asked Peter, raising our hands.

"Yes," she said. "As soon as we are back at the office. Get in."

The ride from the landing pad to the FBI office was completely normal, which irritated me more than I could express. I wanted the whole world to share my anxiety over Samarie's fate, but instead people went about their business as if it were just another day.

Periodically, Agent Patel would say something cryptic and brief into her headset, often accompanied by nodding her head.

"Can you at least tell me what's happening?" I pleaded with her. "It's been almost a half an hour since we heard from Samarie."

Turning to face me, she replied, "Ms. Wilson, there's nothing to tell. Our people are searching for her right now. As soon as I know anything I can report, I promise I will inform you." Then she turned back to face the windshield.

"This is so frustrating," I said to Peter. "I feel completely impotent. I don't like not knowing what's going on."

"I know how you feel. Once Jackie started her bid for Senate, she hasn't said more than five words to me on any given day. I was completely surprised when she showed up at my hospital room the other day. It was the longest conversation we'd had in over a year."

"I'm still trying to figure that one out. What did she say to you?"

"We talked mostly about her campaign. She's sunk more than thirty million dollars of her own money into winning this election. She kept accusing me of trying to scuttle her chances of becoming Senator."

"Are you?" I asked.

"What? How could you ask me that? I thought you understood why I came forward."

"You have to admit, though, that coming forward a week before the November elections is pretty suspicious timing. If this story hits before tomorrow, not only will it destroy Jackie's chances of being elected, but it will also make the President, Vice-President, and every Senator, congressman, and cabinet member who ever supported biotech look like a bunch of butchers. This is the biggest political disaster in modern history. This is going to make a lot of very powerful people extremely unhappy, especially the day before the election. The timing couldn't be worse."

We arrived at the FBI building, and Agent Patel escorted us up to yet another little blank room. There were coffee and sandwiches waiting. I thought about having a sandwich, but my stomach was still in knots over Samarie. Peter, on the other hand, helped himself to the food with gusto.

With food in his mouth, he said, "You're right. This is going to make every administration back to the Eighties look like fools and criminals for supporting biotech. There have been people warning against just this sort of disaster for years, but no one took them seriously. You're completely off base as far as my timing is concerned, however. I'm not trying to scuttle Jackie's chances at being elected. If she had stayed CEO of Verigro, maybe she could have staved off this story, fought it in the courts, spun it in her favor. As a Senator, she can't afford even the appearance of impropriety. Her constituents would crucify her. It doesn't matter if the story comes out before or after the election. This is going to destroy her political career one way or another."

"Not only her," I said. "Errol is going to take a huge hit for this."

"Why? I thought you said he didn't know about BioStar and WBS."

"I…" I began. "You know, you're right. Apart from being part of the Iranian conspiracy, he couldn't have possibly known about the toxicity of BioStar. Not unless Jackie told him."

"She wouldn't have done that," replied Peter. "She's been spending the last three years covering it up."

"Then why the hell did he send those police goons to kill us in that warehouse?" I wondered aloud.

"Who says he did?" asked Peter.

"He was the one who chose where to meet. I had no idea where we were going, and neither did Nick. That leaves you and Errol, and I seriously doubt you had anything to do with that ambush."

"Thank you," he said.

Then something occurred to me, but I dismissed it almost as soon as it came. "No," I said aloud.

"What?"

"No, it couldn't be her," I said.

"Who?" demanded Peter.

"Marcy, Errol's assistant. He asked her for the address. She's the only other person who knew where we would be. You think she's working for Jackie?"

"Why not? Everyone else in the whole damned world seems to be."

"Holy shit," I said.

"What now?"

"Errol isn't behind Samarie's abduction. Someone is setting him up." I reached for my phone.

"What are you doing?" demanded Peter. "You're not going to interfere with Samarie's rescue, are you?"

"Errol needs to know what's going on," I insisted.

"Why, damn it?"

"Samarie is Errol's daughter."

Chapter Forty-Two

"Mr. Foster's office. May I help you?"

"Hello, Marcy," I said coldly. "This is Lotte Wilson."

Marcy was ever cheerful. "Hello, Ms. Wilson. How can I help you today?"

"I need to speak to Errol. It's an emergency."

"I'm sorry, Ms. Wilson. Mr. Foster is out of the office today. I can let him know you called, if you like."

I could feel my frustration rising. "No, I don't like. I already tried his mobile, and he isn't picking up. This is very urgent. I need you to put me through to Errol now."

"With all due respect, Ms. Wilson, I have the same number for his mobile as you do. If he isn't picking up for you, I would imagine I would have about as much luck. May I take a message? I promise he'll get it as soon as I hear from him."

"God damn it, Marcy," I snapped. "I don't know what kind of game you are playing, but I swear, if anything happens to Samarie, you'll be the first person I come after!"

Peter took the phone away from me and disconnected the call. "What the hell is wrong with you?" he demanded.

"That bitch was playing with me. She knew damned well why I was calling, and she still acted all innocent and professional. She's keeping Errol from me."

"You don't know that. You have a hypothesis that she's in on it, nothing more. It's possible she just didn't know how to get in touch with him."

"But…" I tried.

"And besides," Peter said, interrupting me, "even if she's really as evil as you say she is, the mastermind behind all our troubles, tipping your hand to her like that was not a good choice."

"I never said she was the mastermind," I said sheepishly. "I just said she's working for Jackie."

"Which is a total blind guess, isn't it? She may be completely innocent. Did that ever cross your mind?"

"But…" I tried again.

"Look," he said softly, "I know you're worried about Samarie, and you're pinning your hopes on Errol to magically ride in and save the day."

"No, I…."

"Why don't you just let George and the other agents do their jobs? It's possible that Samarie is safe right now, and we just haven't learned about it yet."

"It is also possible," I said without looking at him, "that we were too late, and…."

"You don't know that." He lifted my chin to make me look at him. "You don't. You're stronger than this, Charlotte. I've known you a week, and I already know that about you. After all the shit that we've been through, now is not the time to lose it."

"Oh, yeah?" I challenged. "When exactly will it be okay to lose it? After Samarie's dead? Will it be okay then?"

"Samarie is not going to die."

"You don't know that," I said, repeating his words.

Peter stepped away from me and went to the side table where the food was. "Here," he said, handing me a sandwich, "eat this. You need to keep your strength up. I'll see if they can bring in a cot. There's nothing you can do until George comes back anyway."

"Yes, there is," I said. I picked up the again phone and dialed.

"What are you doing?" he asked.

The phone rang and rang. I hung up and called again. "Calling Errol's mobile."

"Charlotte," he began.

"No," I shouted. I dialed again. "I'm not giving up. Samarie is out there, and I don't know if she has a sandwich or a cot or anything. All I can do right now is to try to reach her father, so that's what I'm going to do."

"I don't see how that's going to help," he said.

No answer. I dialed again. "It's going to help me."

"Fine. Go ahead and waste the battery, so when Samarie calls next time, you won't be there to take the call."

That stopped me cold. I looked at the phone and checked the battery level. It was down below half. He was right. I needed the phone to be working.

I reached for the disconnect button. That's when I heard a distant voice say, "Hello?"

"Oh, my God. Errol," I said, bringing the phone to my ear.

There was a lot of noise in the background. "Lotte? Have you been calling me?"

"Errol, listen to me," I said. "I need your help."

"All right. What can I do for you?"

"It's Samarie. She's been kidnapped."

"Oh, my God, Lotte, I'm so sorry to hear that. I saw something on the newsfeed about a kidnapping, but I...."

"There's more, Errol. You might want to sit down for this."

"Lotte, just tell me. No more games."

"You have to help me get Samarie back, Errol."

"Why me?"

"I've been thinking about how to tell you this for years, and this is definitely not the way I imagined. She's... she's your daughter, Errol."

"What was that?" he shouted. "I couldn't hear you. What about Samarie?"

"She's your daughter," I yelled into the phone.

It was suddenly quiet on Errol's end. "This is some kind of joke, right?" he said finally.

"No, I swear it's true."

"How...?" he stammered.

"It was right before you sent me to Iran, remember? I convinced you to let me go."

"Yeah, you were very convincing all right." He paused. "But I thought Warren was the father."

"No, it's really you," I confirmed.

"Why the hell didn't you tell me sooner?"

"Because I didn't, okay? I'm telling you now. And right now, Samarie needs your help."

"My help? What do you expect me to do?"

"I don't know, Errol. I'm stuck in the FBI headquarters in Chicago, waiting to hear anything about her. So far, there's been nothing. You're in Chicago now, aren't you?"

He hesitated. "No, I'm out of town. But I will get someone working on this right away. Just sit tight, Lotte. I'll do everything I can to help get Samarie back. I promise."

"Thank you, Errol," I said, but he was already gone.

Chapter Forty-Three

The first thing he said as he entered the room was, "I'm sorry, Charlie."

"Oh, God, George, she's not…."

"No, no, nothing like that. We searched the entire building from top to bottom. We didn't find Samarie anywhere."

I let out a deep breath. I had been holding it for hours. "But she could still be all right, couldn't she?"

"We hope so," he said.

"What do we do now?" demanded Peter.

"There's nothing much we can do but follow our leads and hope the kidnappers call in," George said. "We don't know anything about who has her. We don't have a description of a person or a vehicle. Until we hear from the kidnappers, we have to wait."

"What about security cameras?" I asked. I was grasping at straws, but I had to ask.

"Down for maintenance," replied George.

Peter seemed as frustrated as I felt. "The whole building?"

George shrugged. "We talked to the technician who pulled the DVRs. He was there on a regularly scheduled maintenance stop to swap the drives. It was just a coincidence."

"I don't believe in coincidences," I said.

They ignored me. "All right," Peter said, "then who owns the building? Maybe that will tell us something."

George checked his notes. "Star Overland Holdings. We're still checking them out."

"Star Overland?" laughed Peter. "I can tell you who owns that. Jackie does."

"You've got to be kidding," I said.

"Well, not directly, but think about it. 'Star Overland.' 'BioStar over land.'"

George pulled out his phone and stabbed at it. "Martinez here," he said. "Check Star Overland ownership for connections to Jackie Hughes. Thanks." He put his phone away. "All right, we're checking. But even if she does own it, it doesn't prove anything."

Peter looked at George. "Sure it does. If Samarie was in a building owned by Jackie, that meant the kidnappers—whoever they are—were comfortable taking her there. Maybe Jackie has an office there. I don't know."

George frowned. "Aren't you a little eager to pin this on Jackie Hughes?"

"Why not? She's been the moving force behind this whole mess for at least thirteen years. I mean, think about it. Warren was going to see her in Milwaukee when he was sidetracked to Bannockburn and ambushed. Whoever killed him took Samarie. Then they take Samarie to a building that is owned by Jackie that just happened to have all its cameras down for maintenance. You really think that it wasn't Jackie all along?"

"Unfortunately, hunches aren't proof. Until we…."

George's phone beeped. He picked it up off the table and put it to his ear. "Martinez." He listened for a moment. "Come with me," he said to Peter and me as he stood. We followed him out of the room and down the hall into a common area. Everyone was crowded around a large monitor on the wall. A woman noticed us come into the room.

"Run it back," she said.

Someone pointed a remote at the monitor and pressed a button or two.

Errol appeared on the screen, dressed in a suit, looking haggard. The network logo showed FMN, and the caption at the bottom of the screen read, "Errol Foster makes appeal for kidnapped girl."

"Ladies and Gentlemen, I have just learned of a terrible series of events. An eleven-year-old girl named Samantha Marie Boyd, who also answers to Samarie, has been kidnapped—twice." A picture of Samarie appeared in an inset next to Errol's head. "First, a man named Warren Boyd—who was thought to be Samarie's father—

kidnapped her from her home in Montana and brought her to Bannockburn, Illinois, where Mr. Boyd was killed a few hours ago for reasons thus far unknown. Whoever killed Boyd then took Samarie to Chicago, where she is presumed to be now. The FBI is searching for her as we speak.

"Samarie is also the daughter of one of FMN's reporters, Charlotte Wilson. She has asked me to step in and make an appeal for Samarie's safe return. Therefore, I am offering a reward for the return of Samarie Boyd. Two million dollars to the person or persons who can return Samarie to her mother unharmed, no questions asked. Call it a ransom, call it a reward. I am not working with the authorities, and I don't care what you do after you return Samarie. Just bring her home, please.

"You can return her to any FMN office, anywhere in the country. A map of our locations is available on our website. The web address should be on your screen as I speak. I promise FMN won't reveal your identity to anyone.

"This is a limited time offer. You have twenty-four hours to bring her to us. After that, I will offer the money to anyone who can bring you to justice, dead or alive. You have twenty-four hours to make the fastest two million dollars in your life. After that time, your life won't be worth two cents. It is in your best interest to bring Samarie back now."

Errol looked at his watch. "It is now 9:04pm Central Time on Monday night. You have until this time on

Tuesday to produce Samarie. Do the right thing. Bring her back to us. Thank you." And he turned away from the cameras, refusing to answer any questions.

George turned to me. "What the fuck was that about?" he demanded.

Everyone turned to look at me.

"I… may have called Errol and told him that Samarie is his daughter."

George gaped at me. "Say that again?"

"I called him and told him that Samarie was kidnapped and that she is his daughter. I thought he could help. I had no idea he was going to do that," I said, waving at the monitor.

"Is she?" asked George. "Is she his daughter?"

"Yes," I said simply.

"Charlie, do you understand that this is not going to help? We want to catch these bastards."

I could feel my frustration building. "If it will bring Samarie back, I don't give a shit what happens to the people who took her. Let them go to Aruba and sip margaritas for the next thirty years. I just want my daughter back."

One of the agents stepped forward and said, "Martinez, we're already getting calls asking for confirmation of this story. What should we tell them?"

"Beats the hell out of me," he said, running his hands through his hair. "Tell them it's true, I guess." He turned back to me. "And you. Give me your damned phone."

"No! What if Samarie calls again?"

"Then she'll talk to one of our agents. Hand it over." I hesitated, but George said, "Charlie, hand over your phone or I swear I will lock you up. I don't want to, but I will."

Peter reached into my bag and handed the phone to George. "Here," he said.

"What are you doing?" I demanded.

"Complying with an order from the FBI. You might want to take the hint," he replied.

It took me a moment to realize what was going on. I turned to George and said, "There, damn you. Are you happy now?"

"No," George said. "I'll be happy when Samarie is home safe and we can sort this whole mess out." He took me by the elbow and led me back to the room with the sandwiches. "Stay here. And don't make any more phone calls without my say-so. Got it?"

"She won't," Peter said.

George nodded and left.

"What the hell was that about?" I asked, confused. "Why did you give him your phone?"

"You're going to need yours. Besides, George didn't lock the door. We're getting out of here."

"We… we can't do that," I said.

"Why not?" asked Peter. "No one is paying any attention to us anyway. I say we just walk out the door."

"And go where?"

"I have an idea," Peter said.

Chapter Forty-Four

Even at nine o'clock at night it was surprisingly easy to find a taxi in Chicago. George must have eventually figured out that we left, and I felt bad for escaping from his custody, but Peter was right. We couldn't continue to sit around and do nothing.

The taxi driver almost fell out of his chair when we told him we were headed for Milwaukee. He warned us that the fare would be well over three hundred dollars. The grin on his face was worth every penny when we said that would be fine. At least someone was having a good night.

We told the driver to keep his speed down—we didn't want to get pulled over—but at that hour it still only took us a little over an hour and a half to get to Whitefish Bay.

On the ride Peter explained his plan. I didn't know if it would work, but he assured me that everything would be fine. At that point I was willing to try anything.

The taxi stopped in Peter's driveway next to his BMW. It was about eleven o'clock. I waited with the taxi driver while Peter went to fetch the fare. He came out with a wad of twenties—I guessed it was over four hundred dollars' worth—and handed it to the driver. And when Peter told him to keep the change, I thought the poor man's head would split in half from the smile on his face.

We went up the walkway and entered through the front door.

"How did you get in?" I asked. "I thought you didn't have your keys with you."

"There's a code-pad built into the lock," he said. As we entered, he said, "God, what a mess!"

"Yeah, that guy really did a number on this place."

He wandered around, inspecting the carnage, turning on lights as he went. He would tsk or gasp as he entered each room.

"This is ridiculous. How the hell was he supposed to find anything this way?"

"I wondered the same thing. I'm still trying to figure out how you found your cash that quickly."

"They left it on the floor," he said, pointing to a side table. There were bills scattered everywhere. "If they were trying to make it look like a robbery, they did a really shitty job."

Peter headed upstairs, and I followed closely behind him. I noted a pool of blood and a tooth where the man with the gun had lain.

"Peter, this house isn't secure. I've broken in twice, and other people have as well. Are you sure it is a good idea to stay here tonight?"

"Good point." There was a code pad for the alarm on the wall outside his office. He tapped a quick staccato sequence and the thing beeped. Then he went into his office and took down a picture. He pushed on a segment of wall, which clicked open. A safe was behind the wall. After a moment, the door swung open, and he reached inside to pull out some papers. "Here you go," he said, handing them to me. "All the proof you could want."

I looked over the documents. All of them had "Confidential" watermarked prominently across the page. They were reports. I couldn't understand half of it, but the abstracts and conclusions were clear enough: there was a statistically significant correlation between exposure to BioStar and the occurrence of WBS.

"I don't know if it is going to be enough," I said as I followed Peter downstairs to watch him lock up.

"It'll be enough," he said. He took the papers from me and reached for my hand. "Are you joining me?"

"Peter, I'm flattered…" I began.

"All right," he said, and he kissed me on the cheek. "Let's go see what the state of the guest room is."

Chapter Forty-Five

I finally fell asleep at 3:00am and tossed and turned the rest of the night. And all the while, I dreamed about Samarie. I would run toward her, but no matter how fast and how far I ran, she would always slip away from me. By the time Peter tapped on my door at 7:00, I had probably managed to get an hour's sleep, and I was completely exhausted.

"I hope you like your coffee black," he said.

I rolled out of bed and stood. I was only wearing my bra and panties, but I didn't care that Peter was standing there. When this was all over, he could look at me naked all he wanted.

"Black is fine," I managed. He handed me the mug, and I drank it greedily.

"Good," he said, "the milk was disgusting." He walked out of the room, saying, "Go take a shower and get dressed. We have to go soon."

I showered quickly in the guest bathroom. For some reason, Peter had some very feminine shampoo and soap in the shower. I didn't want to know why. Either way, it felt good to be clean after sleeping in jail the night before last.

I dried my hair as best I could, dressed in my dirty clothes, and wandered downstairs.

Peter looked at me and made a face. "No offense," he said, "but you look like hell. You can't be on camera like that. Hold on a minute." Before I could argue he ran up the stairs two at a time. I checked myself in a mirror. My clothes were filthy and wrinkled. I did look like hell.

"Are you a size four?" Peter shouted down the stairs.

"You're sweet. Try size eight," I called back.

A moment later, he came down the stairs carrying a white blouse, a blue skirt, and a very lacy pair of purple panties. "This is all I have in your size. I wasn't sure if you needed the panties. Women…."

"Uh, no thanks. But I'll take the other stuff." He handed it to me, and I quickly changed into the clothes. I wanted to ask what he was doing with women's clothing in a variety of sizes. Even if he had women over all the time, why would there be clothes here? I decided to let it go. It wasn't relevant at that point.

"Ready," I said.

"Okay," Peter replied, checking his watch. "Make the call, and we'll go."

My phone was fully charged, but I had lost my headset with the camera somewhere in all the craziness. I dialed Errol's mobile number and prayed he would answer.

He picked up on the third ring.

"Lotte, I haven't heard a thing," he said by way of greeting.

"That's not why I'm calling. I need a favor."

"Another favor? Now I know you're joking."

"This is no joke, Errol. I'm about to get the story on BioStar, but I need your help to do it."

"What?" he demanded.

"I need you to call the station in Milwaukee and tell them to give me a camera and a live feed."

Errol paused, as if he were assimilating what I just said. "A camera I can understand. What's the live feed for?"

"Peter and I are going to get Jackie to incriminate herself. I want the story to go out before the polls open."

Errol paused again. "This is against my better judgment, but okay. You've got your live feed. What else?"

"Just tell everyone else to stay away. After all the shit I've been through, this is my story. Can you live with that?" I asked.

"Fine. BioStar is all yours. I'll make the call. And I'll contact you as soon as I hear about Samarie."

"Thank you, Errol. I can't tell you how much I appreciate you backing me up."

"Make this work, Lotte. I told you before, you've bet your career on this story. If you screw it up, you're done."

"Fair enough," I sighed. There was a click as Errol terminated the call.

I looked at Peter. "We're in business."

"Lock and load," he said.

"Lock and load," I repeated quietly.

Chapter Forty-Six

True to his word, Errol had called ahead to the station. I was able to get the equipment I needed, and the live feed was set up and waiting for my signal.

Jackie's campaign headquarters was only about five miles from the station. We arrived at about 8:30am, and the place was already swarming with people. I was surprised to see that very few of them wore masks and gloves. Evidently these people didn't feel very strongly about catching WBS. I didn't take a lot of time to think about that. I had other things on my mind.

Peter parked near to the headquarters. He grabbed the BioStar reports and we dashed across the street. I looked through the windows. The place was packed, which is exactly the way we wanted it. We walked inside as if we owned the place.

Blue and white "Hughes for Senate" posters were everywhere, and everyone was wearing a "Vote for Jackie Hughes" button.

A very perky young woman greeted us. "Hi," she said, "how can I help you?"

Peter took the lead. "We're here to see Jackie."

"You'll have to talk to the campaign manager about that," she said, pointing to a man who looked to be in his forties talking to a group of volunteers. Then she handed each of us a button. Peter dutifully put his on and I followed his lead.

"Jim Petty," Peter said.

"Should I know who that is?" I asked.

"No, but he knows me." Peter headed directly over to the campaign manager. "Jim!" he said loudly, extending his hand.

"Peter!" cried Jim, shaking Peter's hand. "My God, I heard you were attacked. Are you all right? I thought you were still in the hospital."

"Thanks, Jim. I'm feeling much better now." Peter turned to me and said, "May I introduce a friend of mine, Charlotte Wilson."

"A pleasure, Charlotte," said Jim.

"Hey, listen, Jim, we're here to see Jackie. Can you ask her to give us a couple of minutes?"

"Oh, sure," he said. "I'll go get her."

"Thanks a bunch," Peter said cheerfully, and he clapped Jim on the shoulder.

We followed Jim a few paces behind. He went in through a locked door but left it open. As we waited outside, I could hear him say, "Guess who's outside?"

I put the camera over my ear, connected my phone to FMN's live feed, and nodded to Peter. Here we go.

Peter pushed the door open and stepped inside, with me right beside him.

"Hi, Jackie," Peter said.

Jackie didn't seem at all surprised to see us, which made the hairs on the back of my neck stand up.

"I've been waiting for you, Peter. I heard you were in town. And I see you brought Ms. Wilson. Excellent. I wanted to talk to you both."

Peter and I looked at each other. "How did you know we were in town?" he asked.

"Let's just say a little bird told me. Now, let's get down to business." Jackie sat down again, and steepled her fingers. "What are we going to do about all this unpleasantness?"

I couldn't find the words to respond to this. I could feel my frustration get the better of me, and I said, "Unpleasantness? You call executing my producer unpleasantness? You call murdering my ex-husband and kidnapping my daughter unpleasantness? You are evil, you know that?"

"Those are very strong accusations, Ms. Wilson. I presume you have some reason to believe that I am connected to those crimes. I mean, after all, you are an experienced reporter. You know better than to make unsupported allegations."

This was all wrong. She had me on the defensive, and I was beginning to look like a fool. I wanted to cut the live feed, but I knew that would be worse than continuing with the broadcast. I had to get a hold of myself, turn the tables on her. I took a deep breath and began again.

"It's time people knew the truth, Ms. Hughes," I said.

"What truth is that?" she asked sweetly.

"This," Peter said, holding up the papers. "BioStar."

"I don't know what you think you have there, but there is no 'proof,' as you call it, to be had. There is nothing wrong with BioStar."

"Nice try," I said. "I've seen the reports. They're authentic. And I know all about your conspiracy during the Iranian war. It won't do you any good to deny it. Warren Boyd has already confirmed everything. The story will go out."

Jackie laughed. She actually laughed. "Warren Boyd? Isn't he the man who kidnapped your daughter two days ago? Oh, that's right. I heard he turned up dead yesterday. I seriously doubt anyone will believe anything that Boyd may have said."

"That doesn't change the fact that you are poisoning people with BioStar. It's toxic, and you know it," I said, pointing to the reports in Peter's hand. "The blood of every man, woman, and child who has died of Witko-Byrne Syndrome is on your hands."

Jackie laughed again. "Is that what he told you?" She began laughing so hard she almost fell out of her chair. "That's what you think this is all about?"

"What's so damned funny?" asked Peter.

"Why don't you tell her the real reason you're doing this, Peter?"

"What is she talking about?" I asked. I was beginning to worry. She was too confident, and we were being forced to make it up as we went.

Jackie continued chuckling. "The reason he's coming forward with this 'confession' right now is because I froze him out of the CEO job at Verigro and gave it to Haley Bowen. He's upset because he's not getting my job."

"Is that true?" I asked slowly.

"No!" he insisted. Then I saw doubt cross his face. "I mean yes."

"Which is it?" I demanded.

"Yes, if she wins the Senate seat, Jackie is giving the CEO slot to Haley, but no, that's not why I'm doing this."

"Come on, Peter. Tell her the truth. You've been bucking for my job since I brought you on five years ago."

I turned to Jackie. "You mean, after he finished serving six years in federal prison for covering up your little science experiment in Iran?"

Jackie's face fell just the smallest amount. I took the opening in her guard and went for the kill.

"Why did you hire a convicted felon to be your Chief Operating Officer, anyway? And why did you give him a new identity? Because you're a nice person?"

"I'm not certain you understand..." she tried.

"Oh, I understand perfectly. I think it was because you owed him for taking the fall for you. And what was he covering up? The dissemination of QT wheat, a precursor to BioStar, in Iranian fields. You were doing illegal human trials on the Iranian people in the middle of the war. That's what's referred to as a 'war crime.' Look it up."

"Now just a minute," Jackie tried again.

"But the trials weren't long enough, were they? Because BioStar takes years to accumulate in the body. And when it turns into WBS, it's so far removed from the consumption of BioStar that you have plausible deniability. But not anymore. The FBI is combing through your database right now, and they're going to have enough evidence about the connection between BioStar and WBS to put you away for a thousand years."

"But that's impossible," cried Jackie. "We deleted the database…" Jackie stopped short. "Oh, God," she said, slumping in her chair.

I couldn't believe it. She admitted it. She actually admitted she knew.

"Did you get that?" asked Peter, smiling.

I ignored him. He missed the point completely.

"Where's my daughter?" I asked in a low tone.

"What?" asked Jackie.

"Where's Samarie?" I shouted.

Jackie looked at me in surprise. "How should I know?"

"You took her, you bitch. Now bring her back!" I started walking around the desk. If she wouldn't tell me the truth, I would beat it out of her.

"Why would I take your daughter?" she attempted, but I didn't believe her.

My fists clenched. "Give her back," I growled, low and menacing.

Jackie reached for her desk drawer. I didn't care. Peter, on the other hand, had had enough, I guessed. He grabbed me around the waist and lifted me off the floor.

"Let go of me," I screamed.

"She doesn't know, Charlotte." He dragged me out of the room and pushed me out the door. He closed the door behind him. "She's done. We got her. Let's go."

"But Samarie…" I said.

"We'll get her back, I promise. But that's not the way."

I turned away from him. That's when I noticed the news crew just inside the front doors of the office. An FMN news crew. Anne King was there interviewing Errol. What the hell?

Chapter Forty-Seven

I pushed my way through the crowd, managing to get close enough to hear what was being said.

Errol said, "Jackie Hughes is an outstanding candidate, and I am here to show my support for her bid for the Senate. As I said a week ago, I am proud to give Jackie my endorsement."

Anne held the microphone close to her mouth. "What of the allegations made against Ms. Hughes in Bannockburn yesterday by Verigro Chief Operating Officer Peter Youngs and FMN veteran reporter Charlotte Wilson? They claim that BioStar is directly responsible for Witko-Byrne Syndrome."

"Charlotte Wilson, I'm sure you're all aware, has recently suffered a personal tragedy. Her daughter was kidnapped by her ex-husband, who subsequently committed suicide. The girl is still missing, although we are doing everything we can to get her back. I'm sure Ms. Wilson simply misspoke when she implied that BioStar is dangerous. As for Peter Youngs, so far no evidence has come to light that would support a word of his allegations."

"I have the proof right here," Peter shouted, close enough to my ear to make me recoil. I hadn't noticed him come up next to me.

Errol nodded at the cameraman almost imperceptibly, and the camera swung around to face Peter.

Anne didn't miss a beat. "Mr. Youngs, what proof do you have?"

"This report shows that BioStar has a statistically significant correlation with Witko-Byrne Syndrome."

"Has this report been reviewed by independent scientific peer group?" asked Anne.

Peter's face fell a little. "Well, no. It's unpublished."

"So what you have is unsubstantiated. Do you have any verifiable evidence?"

"Yes," I interjected. "Jackie Hughes just admitted on a live television feed to knowing that BioStar is toxic. Every Foster Media viewer was a witness to it. If that isn't evidence enough, I don't know what is."

This time, Errol spoke up. "What live feed, Charlotte?" he asked. "I'm not aware of any live feed."

"What?" I cried. "Errol, you assured me that I would have a live feed. How could you do that?"

"I'm sorry, but we must have misunderstood each other. I never gave permission for any live feed."

That was all I could take. "You bastard! You double-crossed me!"

"I don't understand what you are talking about, Charlotte," he said. "I understood this morning that you had decided to retire from Foster Media because of your distress over the recent circumstances."

I stood there, open-mouthed. I almost shook my head, thinking that I hadn't heard him correctly. "Why are you doing this, Errol?" I asked, almost inaudibly.

"You have my deepest sympathies for your troubles, Charlotte," he said, using my name for the third time. He must have wanted everyone to know exactly who I was. "I just wanted to let you know that I understand how distraught you are, and I won't hold any of your ranting against you."

I wanted to grab Errol by the throat and strangle him right there on camera. Instead, I turned and faded into the crowd.

As I emerged from the mass of people, I could hear someone shouting just outside the front door. I turned to look. George was coming in through the door wearing a black bullet-proof vest with the letters FBI emblazoned across it.

"Secure all these people. I want statements from all of them," he told two other officers, who were carrying small but very lethal-looking machine guns. "You two, go find her." Two agents raced past me and went directly to Jackie's office.

George spotted me and came directly toward me. "You're out of your mind, you know that?" he said.

"I may be out my mind, but I'm guessing you got my fax."

"Oh, I got it all right. It was enough for a warrant."

I heard shouting coming from Jackie's office. Curious, George and I ran over to see what was going on.

Jackie had a gun to her head. The two agents had lowered their weapons and were trying to calm her down.

I had just enough time to activate my recorder before she pulled the trigger. The BOOM was deafening in the small office. Jackie crumpled to the floor.

"Oh, my God," I gasped.

"Cut the feed," I heard Errol shout to the cameraman. "Cut it!"

George shoved me out of the way. They slammed her door closed and proceeded to ignore me.

Chapter Forty-Eight

"I don't know how much good this is going to do you," I said, handing over the memory card, "but here's her confession."

George took the small chip from me, slipped it into a coin envelope, and marked it as evidence.

"Are you going to be all right?" George asked softly.

"No," I said simply. "When Jackie killed herself, my only link to Samarie died with her."

"Don't talk like that," he said. "You don't know that. After that stunt that Foster pulled, the kidnappers have a big incentive to keep her alive."

"Don't treat me like a civilian, George. I know the statistics. Most kidnap victims are dead before the first ransom call comes in."

George began pacing in small circles. "You can't lose hope, Charlie. Not now."

"No? Why not?" I demanded.

"Because as long as there is a possibility that Samarie is alive, she needs you to be strong."

I scoffed. "Nice speech. Do they teach you that in FBI school?" I began spinning in my chair.

I looked over to see Errol and Anne conferring. I wondered what they were discussing. I had thought that Errol would be worried sick—after all the difficulties he had gone through to produce an heir, I hand him one on a silver platter, and now she's gone. But there he was, having a laugh with one of the co-conspirators.

I began to think. Errol had just shut me down, made me look like a fool, and destroyed the credibility of the BioStar story. Why the hell would he do that? He'd been as affected as anyone by WBS—he'd lost at least two children and two marriages to it—so why would he kill the story?

I couldn't think anymore. My brain had turned to mush.

I wished Nick were here. He would know what to say. He would understand what I was going through, what I was thinking. We had been friends for years. I hadn't really thought about him since he… died, but now it all came rushing back.

It had always been Nick and me since before Iran, a team. Woodward and Bernstein.

And then it hit me.

"Follow the money," I said softly.

"What?" asked George. "Have you heard a single thing I've been saying?"

"Excuse me," I said, standing. "Actually," I said, changing my mind, "you might like to hear this. Come with me." I stood up and weaved my way through the crowded room to where Errol and Anne sat.

Errol looked up at me as I approached. He was speaking to someone on the phone. I heard him say, "I'll call you back."

"Insider trading," I said. It was an accusation as much as a statement.

Errol looked at me blankly. "What?"

"When did you find out?" I asked.

"Find out what?" he demanded.

"That BioStar causes WBS. It sure as hell wasn't when I told you that day in your limo. You knew before, didn't you?"

"Lotte, you're tired and worried and depressed. You don't know what you're saying."

I laughed, but without any humor. "Nice try. But I know perfectly well what I am saying, and so do you. If the BioStar story hits before you can get out of Verigro stock, you'll lose billions. Considerably more than the measly two million you offered for Samarie's life. You've been trying to kill this story since the beginning, haven't you? Nick and Warren died to keep your secret, didn't they? How many more will die while you dump your Verigro stock?"

George grabbed my arm. "Charlie, what are you talking about? You can't go around accusing people of conspiracy and murder. Errol's a public figure. He can sue you for defamation, and I promise you, he'll win." He began tugging at me, pulling me away.

"No, it's all right," Errol said. He stood and faced me. "I'd like to say I don't know what kind of man you think I am, Lotte, but I'm pretty certain I do. You've painted me as the villain of this piece." He shook his head sadly. "You're a good reporter, but you never did see the big picture, did you? Not when I asked you to marry me, and not now."

"Explain it to me," I challenged him.

"Have you bothered to have your official friend here," he said, gesturing to George, "or anyone else check my recent stock sales? I haven't sold any Verigro stock, not for weeks. There isn't any way I could have dumped that much stock without affecting the price. If you want to talk to my broker, I'll give you his number."

Errol took a step toward me, but I recoiled into George. Errol stopped and stared at me for a long moment.

"The reason you're retiring is because you've lost your touch. You've always had your facts straight, but not with this story. You're too close to it. It's time to let it go."

I opened my mouth to reply, but closed it again. There wasn't anything I could say.

Errol smiled softly. "I'm sorry, Lotte." He turned and went back to his chair, took out his phone, and made a call.

I turned and walked away, followed by George. I found a comfortable looking chair and flopped into it.

"Maybe he's right," George said.

"Don't you start with me, George. I wasn't wrong."

George looked at me for a long moment. Then one of his minions caught his eye, and he was gone. I was alone.

I looked over at Errol again. He was on the phone, lost in his own little world. I hated that he could be so cavalier when I was a wreck. I hated him.

Which made it terrible timing for Peter to come speak to me.

"Charlotte?" Peter said from behind.

"What do you want?" I snapped.

"I just wanted to…"

I interrupted him without looking at him. "When the hell were you going to tell me the truth?"

"The truth about what?" he said innocently.

"The truth about why you were coming forward now. Is this really about you being slighted out of the CEO spot?"

"No! Of course not. I came forward because I care about all the people who are dying from WBS. That's the truth."

"Is it?" I asked. "I'm a very good judge of people, Peter—or at least, I thought I was until I met you. Jackie had absolutely no reason to lie at that point, especially when the truth would serve just as well."

"You can't seriously be taking Jackie's word over mine, can you?"

"Actually, yes I am. You've been lying about who you are and what you care about for the last five years, probably longer. What difference would one or two more lies make?"

"I care about you, Charlotte. Can't you see that?"

"Peter, I'm touched by your gesture of sincerity, but I don't buy it. What I buy is that you were motivated by greed and ambition, so you pulled all of us into the middle of all this stupid corporate infighting. I appreciate that what you did was ultimately for the good, but I can't get past your motives to destroy a professional rival."

"So that's it? You're done?"

"Pretty much," I said. I still hadn't looked at him and didn't plan to. Instead I stared out the window.

I could hear his footsteps moving away. When I was sure he was gone, I put my hand over my eyes and sighed.

Suddenly, across the room, Errol stood and cheered. "They've found her!" he crowed. "They've found her!"

I sprinted across the room. "Is it Samarie? Where is she?"

"Come on," he said. "You can ride with me!"

I hesitated. Errol was an accomplished liar, and if I was right about him, he had arranged the murder of too many people for me to trust him now. This could be a ruse to get me alone to kill me too. Or maybe he was telling the truth. Could I even tell if someone were being honest anymore? It didn't matter. Samarie came first. We ran out to his SUV, and hopped in.

"Where are we going?"

"The Milwaukee studio," he said.

"Here?" I asked, surprised. "Why would they drop her here? She was in Chicago."

"Who cares? She's safe."

I couldn't argue with that.

Then I had a sinking feeling in my stomach.

"You can't tell her," I said.

"What? What are you talking about?"

"You can't tell her you're her father."

Errol stared at me for a long moment. "Why not?"

"Why not? She just lost Warren and she's been kidnapped. She's had enough shocks for a while. Please, I'm begging you. Give her time."

Errol considered for a moment. "All right. But she has to know soon."

"Soon, but not today. Agreed?"

Errol was silent. I took that for assent.

With the studio so close, we were there in ten minutes. I had my door open before the SUV came to a stop. Errol was right behind me.

"Where is she?" I demanded of the security guard.

"Station Manager's office," he pointed as I ran by.

We followed his finger to the office where Samarie was. I burst in the door, and there she was.

"Mommy!" she cried and rushed toward me.

"Oh, my God, baby. I'm so happy to see you!" I wrapped my arms tightly around her. My left arm complained, but I didn't care. I had my baby with me again.

I cried. Samarie cried too. I have no idea what Errol did.

When my mind worked again, I asked her, "Are you hurt? Did they hurt you, baby?"

"I'm fine, Mommy."

"I'm so happy to hear that. I'm never letting you out of my sight again."

"I wouldn't count on that," Errol said, almost too low to hear.

I considered glaring at him, but I didn't want him to ruin this moment.

"Mommy," Samarie said. "I want to go home."

"Right away. We'll leave right now."

"Hold on, Lotte," Errol said. "Whose home is she going to?"

"Mine!" I insisted. "She's coming home with me. I'm still her mother, and I have legal custody. Until that changes, she's staying with me."

"I hate to do this, but…" Errol handed me a little blue pamphlet.

I opened it. It was a court ruling giving Errol custody of Samarie.

"Where the hell did you get this?" I demanded.

"When you told me about Samarie, I talked to my lawyers, and…."

"No!" I cried, dropping the pamphlet. "No, I just got her back. You can't do this!"

"It's already done," he said simply. "I'll let you have one hour with her. Then she's coming with me."

"Mommy, what's he talking about?" asked Samarie.

"Nothing," I sobbed. I turned back to her and held her again. "I'm just so glad to have you back."

Chapter Forty-Nine

I t was the shortest hour of my life.

And after exactly one hour to the minute, Errol walked Samarie to his SUV and closed the door.

I was out of a job, and lawyers are expensive, especially when Errol could outspend me ten thousand to one. I had no choice but to accept his custody of Samarie for the time being.

Through some stroke of good luck, Warren had recently changed his will and left the Orchard to Patricia as his future bride. Patricia immediately incorporated and surprised me by asking me to sit on the Orchard's new board of directors. As the "Principal" of The Orchard, Inc., she had been doing a great job keeping everything together in the months since Warren's death. She invited me to come live at the Orchard with her and the others.

I accepted. My only condition: I wanted a broadband internet link and telephones installed before I set one foot inside. Patricia had called me two days ago to let me know that everything was finally ready.

I sat in the small plane, surgical mask and gloves in place. I knew they were absolutely, ridiculously unnecessary, but I kept up the pretense. With Jackie dead, there would be no trial for her, and it would be months or years before anyone found out about the true danger they were in.

I looked around at my fellow passengers and wondered how many would be dead by this time next year. One in fifteen hundred, said the statistics. So maybe everyone on the plane would survive to see another year. Knowing that didn't make me feel any better.

One thing bothered me, though. Errol had had a DNA test done on Samarie to prove paternity. When the hell did he have time to do that? If I could prove that the test had been done when Samarie was "kidnapped," it would be enough to start an investigation into Errol's role in all the craziness that I had gone through. My lawyer told me to drop it, though. I would never have enough money to fight Errol, but until Samarie was back with me, I would spend every penny I could get my hands on to try. My lawyer was working on getting visitation, which was already an uphill climb, and I had to be satisfied with that for now.

I thought about Samarie, and I cried. I had been doing that a lot lately.

I looked out the window and thought I saw the Big Hole River. I'm sure that Samarie would have been delighted to see it again.

For me, it only reminded me of the hole in my soul that was left when Samarie was ripped from me.

Patricia said I would heal in time.

I wasn't interested in healing. The only thing that mattered was getting Samarie back. Foster's billions be damned, he was not going to keep my daughter away from me.

Not forever.

www.ingramcontent.com/pod-product-compliance
Lightning Source LLC
Chambersburg PA
CBHW071236190726
48292CB00007B/2320